A
KNIFE
BETWEEN
THE RIBS

By the Same Author:

The Poor Old Lady's Dead
The Shallow Grave
A Clutch of Vipers
The Gospel Lamb
The Bastard's Name Was Bristow
An Uprush of Mayhem
The Local Lads
Corporal Smithers, Deceased
All the Pretty People
A Time of Fine Weather
A Death in Irish Town
A Little Darling, Dead

A
KNIFE
BETWEEN
THE RIBS

Jack S. Scott

A
Joan Kahn
BOOK
St. Martin's Press
New York

Copyeditor: Erika Schmid

Design by Doris Borowsky

Library of Congress Cataloging in Publication Data

Scott, Jack S.
A knife between the ribs.
"A Joan Kahn Book"
I. Title.
PR6069.C589K6 1987   823'.914   86-27940
ISBN 0-312-00015-4

First Edition

10 9 8 7 6 5 4 3 2 1

A
KNIFE
BETWEEN
THE RIBS

1

One week in the year, the town goes gay. Not gay in the debased sense that has ruined what was once a very happy little word. Not gay as such things go in Gay Paree; but those more lively denizens who still have hair tend to let it down. If they do not exactly clog it in the streets with the Morris dancing teams that come from far and wide, at least they view the antics with tolerance as they go about their mundane business, and they spend a little more in the pubs at night, where, if the wines and spirits move, they will join in the choruses of folk songs jetted through the noses of strangely bearded men with guitars.

Festival Week, they call it. Second week in August. Dreamed up ten years ago by the council, and let nobody blame them for it. Brings a little money to the town, adds a modicum of color. Blame them, if you will, for the canal-side leisure complex that hangs around the ratepayer's neck, a turgid white elephant. Blame them for their tower block that erupted to replace the torn-down, lovely medieval buildings right next door to the part-Norman, elegantly spired parish church in Welby Street. But do not blame them for Festival Week. Nothing wrong with it. Nothing at all. Only the street cleaners moan, shoveling up the old crisp bags and chip papers and worse, far worse; but then, street cleaners are notoriously homophobic. Not without reason.

On the Tuesday of Festival Week a man not in any way remarkable sat in a pub called the Perfect Rest, down in the town center, where Morris dancers refresh themselves with jolly ale in the evening after they have applied footbalm and listen to the strangely bearded singers, come to claim their share of free beer and glory. Around him the buzz of conversation, voices raised to cover the thin croak of the beard currently holding the floor. A few were actually listening, one or two even trying to join in on choruses never heard before.

There was laughter, there was merriment, there were ribboned hats about, and knee breeches, and coats of many colors; but the unremarkable man sat in a blue suit under a flat cap, alone on a settle made for three; withdrawn, glum, perhaps even nervous. And nobody noticed. The locals never dress up, always excepting the council and the mayor when they walk in robed procession behind the official float, all through the town on St. Barnolph's Day.

Two young men came into the pub, wearing woolly bobble-hats. Their jeans were blue, their bright plastic casual jackets zipped up at the front and they sported white canvas shoes. Holidaymakers, one tall, one small, both slim; as unremarkable as the unremarkable man. The small one went to the bar; the tall one to the settle, set beside the big brick fireplace. He sat down and said, "Move up a bit, Dad."

The unremarkable man, who might indeed have fa-

2

thered the lad if he started as soon as he could, reached for his beer and moved it along as he shifted into the corner of the settle, against the wooden arm that flared at the top as wing chairs do. The young man said ta, and sat listening to the guitarist until his friend arrived, bearing two half-pints. He then said cheers and took a deep swig as the second lad seated himself, third man on the settle. Seated, this one also drank deeply. The two glasses came down together onto the table. The first lad said, "Ah. Goes very well, that does. You're sure we've got the right geezer?"

"Better ask him," his friend said, "if you're not sure."

"Only we don't want any mistakes, do we?" The lad was reaching a hand under his armpit, beneath the casual jacket. He turned to the unremarkable man. "Excuse me—aren't you Harry Grebshaw?"

The man started, jerked out of glum brooding. "What? Yes. Who—who are you?"

The hand came out holding a thin knife. Without haste, smiling, the lad slipped this in between the ribs of the unremarkable man, who gasped, and jerked, and looked at him for an astonished second with wide eyes; and died, held upright by the arm and back of the settle.

The young men rose and moved casually toward the door, taking their glasses with them. Nothing to cause comment in that, many people drink outside on fine evenings during Festival Week. The benches come out, the chairs and tables under gaily striped umbrellas. In the doorway they actually bumped into the solid, ape-shape body of Detective Inspector Alfred Stanley Rosher, arriving clad in the durable blue serge suit with the double seat and reinforced cuffs. On his feet the boxy-toed shoes, low on a simian brow the black hat. "Sorry," the tall one said, and they went on their way.

Detective Inspector Rosher grunted, moving on into the bar. The singing, the twanging guitar came into his ears as a formless roaring. Tone-deaf as a carrion crow, he was not one of the locals who gained spiritual sustenance from this week of accordions in all the open spaces, backed by tambourines and the odd drum to discipline a cavorting of knotted calves under velvet breeches, of pan-pipe players, singing guitarists, ticky-tacky fiddlers and hairy ladies rattling collection boxes. If it added to the police burden, it was only by way of increase in the number of reported pocket-pickings, a rise in the D and D arrest rate—matters that ceased to concern him long ago, when he climbed out of uniform and donned the blue serge suit. He entered here tonight with hard little eyes flicking about the bar, engaged on purely routine business. Normal police service is not suspended for a week due to festive knees-up.

Those hard little eyes were seeking and finding the un-remarkable man, still propped upright in his corner of the settle. There he is, the inspector was thinking. Gone to sleep, has he? Because the man's head was bent forward. No doubt about who it was, though, if you were expecting to find him there.

On the public side of the bar the crowd was three, four deep. Rosher shouldered his way through. The landlord, pulling pints and seeing the hat go by, thought what the bloody hell does he want? Brows slightly lowered, eyes suspicious—the inspector had this effect on people in trades where livelihood depends upon police goodwill— he watched as his skilled hands pulled the pump, delivered the well-collared pints. He saw the ape-shape stop beside the settle; saw the leather lips move, speaking above the unremarkable man head-down in the corner;

4

saw the big, fur-backed hand—that hand which, bunched into the Mighty Hammer, in his young days made the boxing Rosher All-England Police Champion (Heavyweight Division) three years running—reach a thick finger, to prod the man awake.

The unremarkable man fell over sideways.

2

"Let us summarize, so far as we can," said the Chief Constable, leaning back in the swivel chair set behind the fine desk in his paneled office with its unsurpassed view of the parking lot. He steepled his fingers. Fine, thin fingers that long ago forgot the feel of the truncheon. "Nobody saw anything."

"That's right, sir," said Detective Inspector Rosher. That is what they had said, all those folk singers and assorted bods in the bar. They had been talking, laughing, listening to the singer. The landlord, his lady wife, the barmaid whose mammary equipment popped the eyes of the unwarned casual—none of them had noted anything untoward. None of them had so much as noted the unremarkable man on the settle, never mind who approached to knife him into limbo amid the jollification.

"Somebody stabbed a man to death in a crowded bar, and nobody saw anything."

"Correct."

All night the inspector had been working. When he

knew the man was dead he immediately closed the pub, sealing all those present inside. Not that he expected it to do much good; common sense said that whoever had used the knife would not hang about, and long, sour experience that the more crowded a place, the more jollity afoot, the less people take notice of anything beyond their own interest.

He used the bar phone to ring the station. By the time sirens wailed and died outside, he was already into the preliminary stage of the inquiry, the general questioning of a suddenly sobered clientele, who stood or sat about trying to keep their eyes away from the dark shape lying on the settle—because a body must not be moved until pronounced dead by a Home Office–approved doctor— and finding them drawn back in morbid fascination.

"Remarkable." The Chief Constable was not pushing out sarcasm. His predecessor, a lion-headed but knock-kneed old tyrant who nearly did for Inspector Rosher at the time of that man's ill-advised grab at the main attributes of a publican's wife—*he* would have scalded it about. He normally did. But the day of the tyrant is done. Most senior policemen nowadays are more urbane, more civilized, most of them able to read without moving the lips. This one could; and he was stating a plain truth. Murder in a public place is by no means unknown; but even so, in a smallish-town pub it is remarkable. And so neatly done, this one. "A professional job, in your opinion?"

"I should think so, sir, yes." One puncture, a clean entry between the ribs and straight into the heart. No sign of the weapon, nobody left in the pub carrying anything more lethal than a penknife, here and there a pair of nail-trimming scissors. Professionals slip away quietly. Amateurs tend to linger. Or they stab in sudden frenzy, giving rise to screaming and a lot of blood.

The Chief unsteepled his fingers. Leaned forward, to pick up his copy of the preliminary postmortem report. No need for him to reread it, he already knew what it said. As did Inspector Rosher, who as first policeman on the spot went with the coroner's officer to the town morgue with the body and watched the grisly process of establishing cause of death—perfectly obvious, one might have thought, but there are legal bindings upon these matters—before going back, with dawn flushing the sky, to the station. The Chief said, his eyes on the buff form because not to look at a paper picked up suggests fidgeting and a weakness of character, "And you yourself were there by appointment with this . . . this . . ." Now he had reason for having picked up the report. He scanned it narrowly. ". . . this Henry Charles Grebshaw."

"I was, sir. He rang me during the afternoon. Confided that he had information to impart." One of my snouts, he was. Had a bob or two out of the Informers' Fund for years and years, Harry Grebshaw.

"Would it have anything to do with that matter, do you think?"

"I doubt it, sir. He never had anything big." And certainly he wouldn't have told anybody he was meeting me. Snouts don't advertise.

"You don't know what he wanted to see you about?"

"Never had a chance to find out."

"Quite. Quite." The Chief shifted his gaze. "And you, Mr. Grinly. You came up with nothing?"

"Not a thing, sir," said Detective Superintendent Grinly; for Mr. Rosher was not the only man here. Apart from this long, lugubrious superintendent, there was another. Chief Superintendent (Rolli) Rawlins, chief by

8

God's bounty of Uniform Branch. Slept in his bed last night. Mr. Grinly, like the inspector, had spent it working and in the same place. Called out by Rosher's phone call, he took over the questioning, the supervising of working policemen, when the inspector left with dead Harry Grebshaw; but unlike Mr. Rosher, who was by now well into overtime, he had only three hours of it racked up. He'd been on night standby. Due off it at six.

"Mm," said the Chief, and steepled his fingers again. "Nothing at all. Prints? Anything of that nature?"

"Million of 'em. Had everything dusted, but . . ." The superintendent shrugged, spreading his hands with the corners of his mouth turned down. They always drooped, but not to that extent. Walk about like that, with your eyebrows raised and all, you could get arrested. On suss, at the very least.

Everybody knew what he was saying. A pub—people crowding, handling all those beautiful shiny glass surfaces, leaning on the bar, moving the chairs, shoving the ashtrays about. Prints on prints on prints. And how do you set about disentangling them? Not a hope. Effort would be made, but not a hope.

The Chief knew, and they all knew that he knew. They all knew he said what he said because—well—why not? Dusting for prints is a routine matter. Mind you, had something nice come out of it, he would have been told by now; but nobody pointed the fact out. Top rank has its privileges.

He spoke again. "Well—we don't have much to go on, do we? Mr. Rosher—you've had a long stretch on duty."

"I'm all right, sir." Sod you, thought Rosher. Don't you go sending me off, putting somebody else on. A cleared murder case brings kudos, and Mr. Rosher was no passer-up of potential kudos. What is the loss of a night's sleep to a man who, over the years, has known much bat-flutter and birdsong on dusk-to-dawn stakeout in places where cats caterwaul among the dustbins, who has seen the sky lighten over High Street bank and back-street warehouse, back to the days when he was not the only bugger around here wearing a black hat. And besides: "I know more about him than anybody. I'd like to stay with it."

This was true. And telling. The background of the late Harry would have to be probed, and who probes a background better than the man who knows something of it?

There was, after all, no other way to approach. Sift all the statements taken at the pub—mass all the dabs together and have them checked, here and by Scotland Yard—these things would be taken care of as routine. Nothing was likely to come out of either. Anything that did show a gleam would be prized out of the direct probe.

This, too, the Chief knew. He said, "How well did you know him?"

A legitimate question. He had not known until Rosher told him this morning that the dead man had been one of the inspector's snouts. In their mutual interest every detective keeps quiet about his snouts, even in shoptalk with other detectives. Every man has his private string; but it would soon vanish if he loosened the lip all over the place.

"I've dealt with him a long time, sir."

"Uh-huh. And you, Mr. Grinly?"

"I was on standby anyway, sir," said Mr. Grinly. "Haven't even got my second wind."

"Good. Good." Yes, the Chief was thinking. Good. It's either you or Fillimore; and if I have Fillimore I can't use Rosher. Put those two together again I will not. Ever. And Rosher is the man with the background knowledge.

10

Detective Chief Superintendent (Percy) Fillimore. A narrow man, and Rosher's archenemy, throughout their careers. Mutual hate sprang out of their eyes the moment they had met, as first-day rookies long ago. It had been springing ever since, deepening to where it interfered with their work when they were put into double harness. Good policemen both, so long as they never met. God in His Infinite Wisdom had fashioned out of harmless clay two baleful policemen locked in the ultimate personality clash. Sometimes, you have to wonder.

The Chief was speaking again. "Well—since you are both working on it already, I suggest you stay with it. Sort matters out between you, will you?" By "sort matters out" he meant pass on to others whatever of existing workloads would suffer from being suddenly neglected, or erupt to get in the way of the new case. Normal practice. As normal as the falling in of the murder team, which would operate mainly from here, in the station. "Thank you, gentlemen. You know where I am if you need me."

Dismissal. The three men filed out, one of them having said never a word.

He said one or two on the way down the stairs. No more were needed. The uniform branch undertakes house-to-house calling, guardianship of site and so on, all within a defined pattern. Here, no house-to-house was called for, no guardian duties except for a copper at the door of the pub, which would drop a little business until allowed to reopen, and then mint a fortune from the crowds who would flock in to gawk at the settle where the dirty deed was done. So having made his statutory appearance in the Chief's parade of principals, Chief Superintendent (Rolli) Rawlins was able to peel off into his office one floor beneath with no great weight added to his

11

normal burden. The other two men went the other way, into Mr. Grinly's office where they sat down.

Mr. Grinly said, "You're right. Pro."

"Uh-huh."

"Neat. Didn't leave a thing to go on. If he had a glass, I wouldn't mind betting he took it with him. Probably into another pub. We can't dust every glass in town."

"Uh-huh." Mr. Rosher was well up with his leader's thinking. A good pro would take his prints away with him, if he had to make some; and he wouldn't be in a pub without a drink—too noteworthy. And he wouldn't wear gloves, for the same reason. Nor would he dump the glass. A dumped glass can be found, wondered about. So: deliver it into another pub. Refilled there—left empty on the bar—dunked into the washing-up liquid and wiped—and you far away.

Yes. Yes—a pro. There was only one glass on the table where Harry died, and that had been matched to him. Nothing else at all. Forensic was working in the pub still, dedicated and scruffy herberts with dome-shaped heads. Bloody hopeless, they were saying. It's just a bloody jumble.

"How long since you last got a whisper from your Harry?" asked Mr. Grinly. Lugubriously, because as the face of Mr. Rosher was dead ringer for a gorilla, and that of (Percy) Fillimore narrow to the point where people, even those who knew him well, considering him in retrospect sometimes could not remember whether his eyes were side by side or one above the other, so Mr. Grinly's features yielded more than most to the force of gravity. Everything went downward.

"Before this?" said Inspector Rosher. "About . . . a year. Eighteen months. Something like that. Heard that he'd straightened out, moved away. Somebody said he got married. Haven't seen anything of him at all."

"And he didn't say what he'd got for you on the blower."

"No. You know what they're like, some of 'em get the idea that we tape all our calls."

"Yeah. Well—look—you must be a bit shagged. Why don't you go and get a bit of kip? We can't do much—I'll get back to the pub, if anything happens I'll give you a bell. Come back, say, lunchtime. Gives you about three hours, how'll that do you?"

Decent man, Charlie Grinly. Mr. (Percy) Fillimore would have said get on or get out, please yourself. "Yeah. Right. I won't bother to go home, I can kip down in the dosshouse."

"Fair enough," said Charlie Grinly.

The dosshouse is a small room behind the CID office, equipped with two narrow camp beds and cheap deal bedside cabinets. It exists for those occasions when a detective may be working night and day for long stretches and must grab sleep as and where he can, close to the action. It is also, and very unofficially, used sometimes after parties, or rows with the wife. On one notable occasion a lady inspector lost rank for threshing about in it with a new cadet. Most of the time it stands empty.

To this small room Inspector Rosher took his durable suit, his boxy-toed shoes, the black hat, and the short-back-and-sides with the little pink tonsure on the crown. It suited him better than return to his house on the hill where the sink glowered with unwashed pots and the fusty clutter increased daily since the fat wife went home weeping to Mother. Like many CID men, he carried a battery razor in the glove compartment of his car and he made no great drama out of sleeping in his underwear.

3

When he awoke, one o'clock by his watch, he washed and shaved at the little sink built into the room. Hot and cold water. No expense spared. He buckled on again the blue serge suit; sat on the edge of the bed to don socks and boxy-toed shoes; stood up; coughed; scratched that small pink tonsure on the crown of his gorilla's skull; combed the short-back-and-sides, checking for tuft sticking up at the back; picked up the black hat; broke wind; and went back to Superintendent Grinly's office. Rapped with hairy knuckles, and went in as invited.

Mr. Grinly sat at his desk, ticking away at things on paper. Bumf accumulated and accumulating around other jobs. He looked up when Rosher entered, saying, "Ah. Little something's come up. Nothing exciting, just a few dog hairs. Found on the settle." He held up a small plastic envelope clipped neatly to the inevitable buff form. "Configuration and general coloration, it says here, suggest Doberman pinscher or similar breed."

"Coloration?" said Rosher.

"Black." Mr. Grinly held out form and envelope. A few black hairs could be clearly seen through the transparent plastic. "Aren't they all black?" He asked because he didn't know; but his main brain was saying: Wish I wasn't lumbered with him. Much sooner have, say, Young Alec Cruse. Anybody, really. You don't even know how to address the old sod, you can't call him Alf, nobody calls him Alf. Nobody calls him anything. Mr. Rosher to his face, Old Blubbergut behind his back. Difficult. Stupid old bastard. And more like a gorilla as the years go by. Cleared a few big ones in his time, though. Can't deny it.

"Hnn. I thought you could get 'em brown," the inspector said. The "hnn" was a sort of grunt. It came from him quite often, to presage speech. "German. Very dodgy." He had a run-in with one once, way back in his beat days. Had its snarling, ravening fangs in his calf before he could get to his truncheon. When he did, and belted it right between the ears, it let go and staggered away cross-eyed, mumbling the canine equivalent of "Ooo—Jesus Christ!"

"Ours is black," said Mr. Grinly. "Had your lunch?"

"Thought I'd look in before I went up."

"Yeah. Well—I'd grab it, if I were you. And then how do you fancy a visit to his wife? See what you can get. She's been to identify; she's been told to stay home or leave word where she is." Asked, he should have said. You cannot tell people where they must be, until and unless you charge them.

"Yeah. Right." The inspector turned away, moving solid bulk toward the door.

"He didn't have a black dog, did he?" Mr. Grinly asked.

"Dunno. Never saw one. He might have had by now."

"Know the address?"

"Pumfrey Avenue."

15

"Right. See you later. If you need me in a hurry, I'll be going back to the pub when I'm clear of this lot."

"Uh-huh." And Mr. Rosher left, on a direct course for the upstairs canteen where he sat alone—few people ever chose to sit with him—ingesting sausage toad and chips, rice pudding with a dobble of jam upon it, and two big mugs of bitter black tea. He then picked up the black hat from the chair beside him, settled it firm and low upon the brow, and left the station.

Pumfrey Avenue, named for an ex-mayor remembered for charitable works and a walleye, is one of several streets that he developed, selling the all-of-a-pattern houses to the town at no more than a fair profit. Signed the contract when he was pissed, or he probably would not have. There was a bit of a fuss that he could do it at all, but quick as a flash he presented an iron lung to the cottage hospital and the rumble died away in mumbling.

Fair little houses, he built. Certainly good enough for the poor, who each were given a strip of front garden too small to keep a cow on, but big enough to grow Brussels sprouts. Those with no taste for sprout growing, and they are the majority in this more enlightened age, plant flowers. Some, of whom the late Harry Grebshaw was one, grow nothing but weeds. They have to keep them trimmed, though. The council comes down upon them if they do not.

Detective Inspector Rosher stood on the step of the Grebshaw house and poked at the bell push. No reply. He poked again. No reply. He doubled the Mighty Hammer and clouted the front door.

It was opened by a smallish woman no longer young but not yet old. Probably younger than she looked. Al-

16

though, of course, she could have been older. She did not smile when she saw him. Not many people did. She said, "If you've been ringing the bell, it's not working."

"Mrs. Grebshaw?" said the inspector, leaving the black hat in situ. Normally, it was snatched off at the appearance in an opening doorway of a female member of the public, and the accompanying beige-toothed beam had been known to knock them back a pace, panic-eyed. They tend, even in this liberated day, to be timid creatures. The voice, too, took on normally the strangulated accent of the railway station announcer or the supermarket girl breaking into *The Best of Mantovani* to summon all those awaiting, like greyhounds in the slips, the first coffee break. But the charm which, he was convinced, radiated from him when he did these things was not awarded to the female appendages of snouts, or other of the little bent.

"Yes." She wore a scarf twisted turban-style on her head and a pinafore over an ordinary house dress. A rather snappy voice, a rather snappy eye, not noticeably swollen by recent grief.

"Police. Detective Inspector Rosher." He flashed his little card.

"Hmph," she said. "They said they'd be sending someone. I was just cleaning the gas stove."

"Uh-huh," he said; and because she was not standing aside: "Perhaps I can come in."

"I don't know why." Definitely snappy. "I don't know what you think you're going to find out. He went out and never came home again. That's all I know."

"Please yourself." The Old Blubbergut bark edged the unstrangulated voice. "We'll give the neighbors a show, if you prefer it."

17

The approach, however couched, usually works. Women hate their neighbors. Her snappy eyes flicked involuntarily over the houses opposite. No curtains were actively twitching, but given the arrival of a strange car and a strange black-hatted gorilla at the door of a woman whose husband—it said so on the midday radio news—had just been murdered, who could tell how many were lurking behind them, eyes beady and lips sucked in? There'd been coppers already collecting her, coppers bringing her back in marked police cars. Heady stuff. She stood aside. Rosher stepped in. "Wipe your feet," she said.

Sod you, he thought, and walked straight on. She made an irritated tut and came after, saying, "The kitchen. We're in the kitchen."

Kitchens are at the back, in small George-the-Fifthian houses. It never varies. The inspector opened the one door facing when you were past the staircase. Ahead of her, he stepped sure enough into the kitchen, where at the table, nursing a cup of tea, sat a second woman. Quite like the first but plumper and more pleasant-looking. Younger, too, if Mrs. Grebshaw was as old as she might have been. The inspector said, "Ah. Good afternoon."

"Good afternoon," the woman said. She wore a neat dress, her hair was neat, her teeth were neat when she smiled. Mrs. Grebshaw spoke, pushing past to get into her kitchen. "My sister."

"Ah." Only now did Rosher remove the hat; but even now, in spite of her pleasantly well-tuned look, he did not bring up the full battery of his strangulated accent and the beige-toothed beam. She was, neat or not, appended to the appendage of a snout.

Mrs. Grebshaw addressed her sister. "Police," she said. "Just when I was cleaning the cooker." Indeed, she had been. The tools stood there on a sheet of newspaper in front of the open oven.

"Oo," said the second lady, widening her eyes. "I think I know you. I've seen you on the telly. Haven't I? Don't tell me—don't tell me—Detective Podger? Bodger?"

"Rosher, madam. Detective Inspector Rosher."

"Something like that, yes. You caught that Avenger— and—you've been on several times. And in the papers. Your photo. Fancy." She surveyed him up and down with a sort of surprised pleasure. "Never thought I'd meet a telly star. You look more like a—" She hesitated, having very nearly said gorilla. "You look—bigger—in real life."

"Hrrrmph," said Inspector Rosher. He'd met the reaction before, in people more closely involved with the newly dead than she was. It gave him no displeasure. She was carrying on, modifying the smile.

"You're here about poor Harry, of course. They said somebody would be coming."

"Shut up, Molly," said Mrs. Grebshaw. She had crossed to her cooker and was folding at the knees. As she sank to the kitchen floor she eyed the policeman. There was, he could see now, a lack of focus, a redness about the eyes. "Get on with it then." She shook cleaner onto a pad and began to attack furiously the inside of the already spotless oven. The whole place was bright and neat. Not a bad housekeeper. Whatever her faults, she had not surrounded her snout with squalor.

"Hrrrmph," Inspector Rosher said again. "Yes. I haven't seen Harry for about a year—"

"Fancy," said the sister.

"—and what we need to know—"

"What do you mean," demanded Mrs. Grebshaw, "you haven't seen him for a year?"

19

The inspector bent stern eyes upon her. He was entirely the wrong man to be bringing comfort to the bereaved, especially when the bereaved turned out to be contemptuously snappy. Snappishness he could not and would not tolerate. Contempt shot the hackles up on his red neck. "What do you mean, what do I mean?"

"Why would you see him? You're not one of his friends. Are you?"

Nothing was going according to decency. Everything was sliding sideways. Did she not know, then, of Harry's business activities, all of them bent, and of his snouting? "We—er—we did a little business, one way and another. Over the years."

"Rubbish," she snapped. "What business?"

"He was an informer, madam." When snapped at, be firm. Very firm. It brought people back into line. "He had extensive criminal associations. He passed information to me. For money."

"Rubbish," she said loudly. "He was a Christian. And don't you shout at me."

"How could he be an informer?" the sister said, widening her eyes again.

"He wasn't," Mrs. Grebshaw snapped, scrubbing away at her oven.

"Yes," said the sister, "but if this gentleman says he was, he might have been. He caught the Avenger."

"He may have caught the Avenger. He doesn't know much about Harry."

"Your husband, madam," Rosher barked, "served several prison sentences—"

"That was years ago." She matched him, snap for bark. "Before he was born again."

"I don't think," her sister said, "we should quarrel over it. That won't do Harry any good."

For Christ's sake, Rosher thought, I'm not here to do Harry good. Nobody's going to do Harry any good, he's dead. Born again? "Madam," he said. "And you—er—madam—I am not here to add to your—er—grief or—er—distress—"

"Will you say what you have to say," Mrs. Grebshaw commanded, "and get out?"

Rarely, rarely did Inspector Rosher find himself baffled. "Flummoxed" is a better word, and it made him uneasy to be so. He had come alone. Normally two call together, to provide backup for each other and to act as mutual witness should any kind of allegation be made; but in cases where nobody is to be accused of anything, when it is merely a question of soliciting help with no thought of its being refused, a man will often go alone. Rosher, ever the loner, preferred it that way.

But going it alone has certain drawbacks. For a start: You have no witness to your conduct and manner; and this, should the visited be hostile and have family present, can be dangerous. Complaint can be made, and will sometimes stick.

Also: Without a warrant, a policeman enters a house only upon sufferance. If, when he is in, the householder in the face of questioning adopts a hostile stance, there is nothing he can do but leave.

He does not always do it. In the case of a familiar male-factor up to his old tricks again, he can be very stroppy. But he will not—dare not—when he comes up, alone and vulnerable, against antagonism from a bereaved woman alone in her kitchen except for a supportive sister, a copper-bottomed witness, do anything but go quietly.

It went against the grain, with the hair on the scarlet nape crackling. To attack Mr. Rosher was to come under attack. Nevertheless, with effort he gathered his dignity.

"In view of the circumstances, madam," he said, "I shall make no mention of obstructing a police officer in the execution of his duty. I shall, no doubt, come back when you have had a chance to think things over."

He turned, slapping on his hat. No need to check the angle; long practice settled it precisely, low on the simmering brow. From beneath the brim little red eyes glared at the kneeling woman, who went on scrubbing away at her oven as though he were already gone. It was her sister who said, "I'll see you out."

He went ahead of her through the narrow passage, where her considerable bosom must have enlarged. As she pushed past him to open the front door—unnecessarily, he could have done it for himself—it squashed softly against his arm. He ignored it. Trouble enough he'd had from bosoms. "Thank you," he said stiffly, moving out onto the step.

"You mustn't hold it against my sister," she said. "She's a bit upset. Naturally."

Was she? She hadn't seemed so. But even his mind had to admit that you never quite know how people will react to emotional stress. Some weep and wail and if they have teeth still gnashable, gnash them. Some rail against God, some become unbecomingly flippant. And women, quite commonly, embark on a flurry of domestic activity. "Hrrrmph," he said.

"She's been a bit funny ever since I got here. I'm sure she'll want to help all she can when she's settled down a bit. I'll have a word with her later, if you like."

"You don't live here?"

"No. No, no, no." She made what was definitely a simper. "I live on the other side of town. Western's Avenue. Do you know it?"

Of course he did. Every good policeman knows every

street in his town. "Uh-huh," he said. She was speaking on.

"She rang me this morning, early. I came straight over. I'll stay with her for a while."

"In that case," he said, "perhaps you will contact me when she seems more amenable. Just ring the station, ask for me personally."

"Oh yes," she said, with a bat of lashes. "Yes. I will."

"I don't suppose you'd know who Harry's been mixing with, who his friends are?"

"No. I haven't seen him for—oh—a long time. We didn't get on all that well."

"Don't you discuss him with your sister?" Most women when they meet discuss their husbands' shortcomings over the teapot. Related women particularly. It's all family.

"I don't see much of her, either. We've never had a lot in common. She's what you might call a bit unworldly. I'm more the earthy type." Once again, a flutter of lashes.

Not altogether surprisingly, even today the occasional woman batted at Rosher. It's all a question of masculine force. Nobody ever called him handsome, even in the days of his boxing glory; but, by God, he stripped to muscle, and women aplenty felt the taste buds stirring at the ringside as he committed his legalized assault and battery, wearing his little shorts. Never mind the bandy legs. And women, too, growing older, are quick to pick up a sign that tells when a man is on his own. The not-quite pristine shirt, a grease spot on the tie . . .

Rosher recognized it. Once, he would undoubtedly have responded. But that was in his day of rampant libido, coming after he finished boxing—while he engaged in it he stayed faithful to a fattening wife; but only, if truth be told, because his old trainer said it weakens

23

you—and lasting until the trauma-triggering moment when he groped a publican's wife. Toward that lady had ramped what was probably his last full erection. Since then, everything was very, very wary. So he kept his eyes stern as he said with limp loins, "Well—thank you. You have been very cooperative." Which is more than I can say for your sister.

"I'll get in touch," she said, "if I think there's anything you ought to know about. But I don't think any of his friends could help you much; I expect they're all Christians."

"Harry's friends?" he said. "Christians?"

"He was born again. They both were. Well—my sister still is, of course."

"Harry was?"

"Yes. Didn't you know?"

"We're talking about the same Harry?"

"Harry Grebshaw. My sister's husband."

"How long's this been?"

"About—a year. Eighteen months. Since that American mission."

"Ha," said Rosher. "Hum. Well—good day, Mrs.—er—"

"Blenkiron," she said; and added with another simper, "I'm a widow."

"Ah," he said. "Humph. Good day." He actually raised the black hat. It did not come right off with a flourish, as was its wont on the doorsteps of the female public, but it went down a little at the front and up a bit at the back. Considerable advance on anything he did for her sister. He bandied down the weed-bordered path, and she stood to watch him drive away before closing the door.

He went around a few more addresses from there, acting, as he normally did, upon his own initiative. Tolerant superiors to whom he was harnessed let him get on with it. He often produced results, nobody could accuse him of wasting time. The less tolerant fumed to a greater or lesser extent, but they came to accept the condition as incurable. Only Chief Superintendent (Percy) Fillimore actually flacked at the corners of the mouth and took to swallowing stomach pills. But then, he did not have to be brought into close contact with Rosher for these things to happen. The mere thought of the man could do it.

Rosher drove about the town knocking on doors behind which dwelt, often with naughties in the cellar, known associates of the late Harry. Nothing much came of it. Some were out, two were in jail. The only one caught at home evinced shock at the sight of him and said he hadn't seen Harry for a year or more. Seen the light, they reckoned. Who were they? Well—everybody. Always was a bit funny, old Harry, and of course he was under the wife's thumb.

This apparent lack of success did not bother Rosher. No policeman expects spectacular progress in the early plodding stage of any investigation. One nugget had come out of it: the astonishing fact of Harry's conversion, attested to from two sources.

Well, well. Who'd have thought it?

4

He arrived back at the station, as he had planned to do, in time for tea. Before going up to the canteen, he reported in to Superintendent Grinly.

Mr. Grinly was still at his desk, but by no means had he been idle. On the contrary, he had worked a full day, and this after a full night. If neither he nor Rosher showed bow-shouldered weariness, this is testimony to the power of the engaged mind over matter. On Mr. Grinly sat the overall responsibility for the inquiry. He would become increasingly lugubrious as time went on, but he would not feel great weariness until the case was cleared. Or shelved. He would sleep as and when opportunity occurred. As would Rosher, who had been known in the past to bullhead his way through three consecutive days and nights without closing a red-rimmed eye.

When he stuck his head round Mr. Grinly's door, that officer said, "Ah. How'd you get on?"

Rosher advanced. Seated himself in one of the small leather chairs grudgingly supplied by the Watch Commit-

26

tee for the benefit of visitors. "Funny woman, that," he said, and ran briefly through the story of Mrs. Grebshaw's noncooperation. Said that her sister was there, staying with her. A Mrs. Blenkiron, lived in Western's Avenue. Finished: "They reckon he'd seen the light."

"Seen the light?" said Mr. Grinly. "Come to Jesus, you mean?"

"That's what they reckon."

"Was he that way inclined?"

"Not so's I noticed. The Blenkiron woman said it, and old Batty Batey confirmed it. He was the only one of his old mates I could get hold of."

He did not have to elaborate. Mr. Grinly was one who exercised tolerance. He found no real joy in being tied to Rosher, but he acknowledged the good points. He had known that all known associates of Harry Grebshaw would be visited and questioned before his inspector returned. He said, "Well, well, well. Batty Batey. Is he still around? How long's your man been bashing the Bible, then?"

"Since the mission, far as I can gather. That's what the sister-in-law says. He seems to have gone straight ever since. I'll find out more when I see the wife again. It's got to be bent."

"Probably, yeah. Funny how it takes some people, though. Wouldn't be the first, would he? It happens sometimes to long-termers in the nick."

"I've known it happen to coppers."

"Yes," said Mr. Grinly. "That's right—who was that daft bastard we had? Took to singing hymns all day, handed out tracts. Even gave 'em to poor sods on stretchers at road accidents. Resigned when they tried to stop him. Big feller, wart on the nose."

27

"Westerhouse," said Mr. Rosher. "Sergeant Westerhouse."

"That was it, yes. What happened to him?"

"Took to flashing, didn't he? Said it was the holiest part of the human body."

"Oh yes. Didn't he go to nick for it?"

"Nuthutch. I think he's still in there."

"That's right, yeah. Poor bastard. Well—gives us something else to go at, doesn't it? We'd better find out where he went. They set up a tin tabernacle or something, didn't they, after the mission lark?"

"Yep. I'll look into that; I have to get back to the wife."

The superintendent indicated papers on his desk. "Reports coming in. Black dogs. Got all the beat men on it." Because the man on the beat knows more than the public realizes about who calls a cat, who owns a budgie, who walks a dog. "All the hotels and boardinghouses, in case somebody booked in with one for the festival. Post office—"

"Post office?"

"Postmen hate dogs. Especially big black ones. Got a hundred addresses here, and more to come."

Rarely, oh so rarely, did Mr. Rosher make a jest. He did so now. "Save a lot of time if you leave my car outside, keep obbo. Sooner or later he'd come along and piss on the wheel."

Superintendent Grinly looked at him in surprise, wondering if it truly was a joke. Decided it had to be. All the lugubrious down-droop bent upward, not so much in tribute to the quality as in acknowledgment of a precious occasion. "Somebody ought to invent something," he said. "Something like an iron boot. Shoots out when they lift a leg and kicks 'em right in the balls. Want to take a couple of hours off?"

"What about you?"

"I'll be going off soon."

"Yeah. All right. I'll give the Blenkiron woman a buzz later, see if she can tell me where Harry sang his hymns. Go and have a word with 'em."

"Right."

All very casual; but this is surface appearance only. Whether the front men are present or in their beds, the team works on, correlating reports, knocking on doors, plod, plod, plod; and beside the front man's bed stands the telephone.

Mr. Rosher went home, but not to bed. Since he intended to be out and about again in the evening, it hardly seemed worth the undressing. He drove up to his house on the hill, scarcely aware by now when he entered of the dust and general clutter. Sitting on the settee in front of the television set, he dozed and napped nicely, as he had known he would, at first with his feet in a soothing bowl of hot water, and, when it grew cold, with bare feet stuck out and the durable blue serge trousers rolled up to the knee. As the wood-carver to his chisels, the cobbler to his last, so the policeman to his feet.

Waking finally from a good dream of boxing, and gilded youth, and eternal glory, he glupped a few times, and arose, and turned off the television. He washed, donned the cleanest of his shirts, retrieving it from the basket where it had been awaiting, with the rest of his washing, transport down to the laundry—he was always forgetting to take in the laundry, until he found himself with nothing clean—and rang Harry Grebshaw's number, getting it from the book.

The sister answered. He knew who it was by a measure of cheeriness in the almost childlike voice that said hello; but he said, "Mrs. Blenkiron?"

"Yes," the voice said, and lifted with a sort of girlish enthusiasm. "Oh—Inspector Rosher. Yes. I was going to ring you, but I thought you might have gone home by now."

"What about?" She, too, had been quick to recognize the voice. No need to tell her he had gone home.

"Pardon?"

"What were you going to ring me about?"

"Oh. Nothing much, really. Just to tell you my sister is more—you know—she's calmed down. Well, not altogether. But she's not so—you know."

"Ah. Good. Perhaps you will inform her that I shall be calling again in the morning." With a witness. And she'd better bloody cooperate. "In the meantime, ask her where Harry—worshiped."

"What, now?"

"Yes. Now." Of course now, you daft cow. What do you think I'm ringing for?

"Hold on," said the cheerfulness, and there followed a short time of silence. She came back. "Hello? Ah—you're still there. My sister says they meet at Pilbeam House."

"Where's that?"

"Oh. Just a minute." More silence. Then: "Hello? On the main road to the city. Just out of town. Beyond Appleton's Garage, she says."

Oh, yes. One of those big old houses. "Will there be anybody there this evening?"

"Hold on."

Why don't you put your bloody sister on? he thought irritably, left standing again in his bare feet and shirt-sleeves with the silent phone at his hairy ear. Too late to command it. This time the phone clunked before she spoke.

"Whoops. Nearly knocked the phone over. Ask for the Reverend Edgar P. Mitten. He lives there."

"Thank you."

"He may be out, she says. It's Festival Week. They have a folk-dancing team staying there."

"Uh-huh. Right. Thank you."

"Not at all." Definitely flirtatious, the girlish voice. "Is that all?"

"Uh-huh."

"I'll see you in the morning, then. 'Bye-ee." The twee farewell heightened the effect of girlishness.

He cradled the phone and padded back into the living room. Ten minutes later he left the house.

A fine August evening. Lucky, for the town and its festival. He drove through the bunting-hung center, where on several corners strolling musicians labored, and utilizing the open areas—in front of the supermarket, around the war memorial, beside the public toilets—pranced the gaily attired dancers, or they stood about recovering breath after the last cavort. Yes, indeed. Chalk one up to the town council.

The main road leading to the big city is a fifteen-minute drive in average conditions from where Rosher's house stands on its hill. It took twenty tonight, some streets being barred to traffic for a week so that people could do in the roadway whatever they felt added to the gaiety, so long as it did not frighten the horses or infringe the law.

Beyond Appleton's Garage, "Last Petrol Before the Motorway"—and that's a barefaced lie—the country begins. Just the three Victorian houses, each in its own extensive grounds, and then the fields, the hills, the woods, seven miles of boskiness lasting, with a vile eruption here and there along the main highway, until you come to the big-city suburbs. Lovely country, and the villages very nearly unspoiled because they lie away down little side lanes where motorists seldom venture, except for the cognoscenti who come to stay in the area for a week or two.

Of the three Victorian houses, two stand behind barbered lawns and neatly fecund flower beds and borders. The third cannot be seen from the road, it lurks behind evergreens and sap-sick trees that stand glum even in fine weather. Of which there is but little in England, so for most of the time they wear the dripping Hammer Films look. This is Pilbeam House. It will be coming onto the market soon, if you want to buy it.

Inspector Rosher left his aging car on the road, electing to walk up the drive rather than clamber in and out, opening the heavy iron gate, closing it behind him, and doing the same thing in reverse when he came out again. A good deal of his work took him into the country, to the charm of which his eye was as blind as his ear was deaf to music; but he never left a country gate open. And he never chased sheep.

Behind the gloomy facade was further gloom. The drive was bordered with rhododendrons which burst in frenzy for two weeks of the year and were bashed back into line by the shocked yews and privets. Beyond these, things were rather better. The drive opened out, forming a forecourt to the solid brick house, and there was a lawn with flower beds. The lawn needed cutting, attention to the beds was obviously desultory; but it came pleasantly to the mind, after the gloom of the approach.

The Victorians built solidly, sometimes even attractively; but rarely could they resist buggering it all with embellishment. This house had gargoyles at the tops of drainpipes, a small tower at one end with battlements, and a heavy, peculiarly squared-off porch with a church-like roof and stained-glass windows. This had an inner door and an outer door; and outside the latter stood Mr. Rosher, hauling away at an old-fashioned bellpull and listening to a jangle from inside.

The inner door opened, revealing a small clergyman. He opened the outer door. "Bless you," he said, beaming.

"Eh?" said Mr. Rosher.

"What can one do for you?" American. Surely American. With All-American teeth. Astonishingly rich, deep voice.

"Police." The usual flash of little wallet.

The beam sobered on the small pink face. "Ah yes. Yes. It will be about poor Brother Henry."

Brother Henry? "I am conducting inquiry into the death of Mr. Harry Grebshaw. I believe you were familiar with him." Not the full mangled-vowel delivery, but a touch of the verbal pomp that comes to policemen standing on doorsteps. It adds weight to the presence, it says that they are not here to sell lavatory brushes. So many nowadays look as though they should be.

"Harry Grebshaw? Yes—yes—we knew him better as Brother Henry. Terrible. Terrible. One of our most devoted brethren. We have heard about it, of course. Do come in." The tiny dog-collared figure stepped aside to clear the way.

"Thank you." The inspector stepped through onto paved flooring. The very small man, who had a receding hairline on a pear-drop shaped dome, closed the outer door and said, "Go on through. Straight ahead." Forget the teeth, his best feature lay in his throat. That voice. Ripe and rounded, touched with mint juleps and *Gone With the Wind*. He used it again as Rosher bandied forward onto tiles. A big, solid hall set with solid Victorian

33

furniture, a broad balustraded staircase curving up to the right. "We'll use the library, if that's okay with you. Second door to the left."

It was okay with Rosher. Why should it not be? He was hardly likely to say no no no, let's use the butler's pantry. The library was as massively furnished as the hall, but carpeted and rugged, with big leather chairs, an enormous settee, and the entire wall surfaces stacked with books, floor to ceiling, which had vine leaves embossed all around the edges and in the center, where it supported a mighty candelabrum. Electrified now, but none the less mighty.

"I have spoken on the telephone to our bereaved sister," the clergyman said as he crossed to the settee. "Do sit down. I believe I was able to afford her some small comfort."

"You have spoken to Mrs. Grebshaw, sir?" Mr. Rosher seated himself in one of the armchairs, facing the wee man who sat with his feet only just touching the rug. Carefully, he placed the black hat on the floor, well back against the leather face of the chair where it would not be inadvertently stepped upon.

"She rang me." The teeth flashed like neon in Las Vegas. "I am, of course, her pastor. Death, we know, is but a passing over. Even so, we make allowance for human frailty when it is visited upon—er—us—so suddenly."

"She is one of your—congregation?" Or whatever you call it.

The cleric worked the teeth again. "Brotherhood. The Brotherhood of Joy. The term is all-embracing, of course, it includes the female—er—sex. Wonderful woman. They both were."

Not Harry. Say what you like, nothing queer about

34

Harry. And nothing wonderful. "How long had he—they—belonged to your—organization?"

"Oh, not organization!" Here was a real chance for the teeth. They took it. There seemed to be more of them than usually germinate in the human gum and they came now accompanied by a rich chuckle, a flutter of tiny hands. "*Dis*organization would be more accurate. We exist in a state of earthly chaos. No, no, we are a Brotherhood, each of us contributing such gifts as have been vouchsafed to us by our Most Mighty Father. In mutual love."

"Ah. Hrrm. How many of you are there, sir?"

"Twelve, of the Inner Brotherhood. Our Mighty Brother, as you know, had twelve disciples. We have another fifty-two sisters and brethren. Here, that is. America-wise, we run into millions. Internationalwise, even more. Over here—it takes a little time for the Word to catch."

'Ah. Hmm.'

"And what can one do for you exactly, suh?" The "sir" was pure Southern gentleman.

"Were any of your—friends—special friends of Mr. Grebshaw?"

"We are *all equal* friends. We coexist in mutual love."

"Uh-hnn. How long had he—er—coexisted?"

"Since our mission of last year. He Came Forward."

"Uh-huh." Rosher remembered the mission. Three days in August, overlapping Festival Week. An American evangelist—the Reverend Makepiece Ewart—ranting and sobbing in the public baths (boarded over, of course) and in a beflagged marquee erected on the open square of the canal-side white-elephant leisure complex. People, planted or simply carried away, crying "Hallelujah" and "Praise the Lord" and a choir in white led by a baritone with a soulful eye and a wide vibrato. Not that Rosher noticed the vibrato

35

or even the baritone. On the only occasion when he attended he was seeking a little dip who he believed would be able to help him in his inquiries. All over the town and in the big city, wherein the Reverend Makepiece Ewart also spread the Word, little dips blessed his name fervently for providing them with the best summer since the royal visit of 1973.

A uniform constable said to Rosher as he left before the finale, "Aren't you going to stay to see 'em come forward? He says, 'who is for Jesus, who is for Jesus, who is for Jesus, come forward, come forward,' and they all start hollering and falling over their feet. Right giggle, it is." But Rosher left. He felt no urge to fall over his feet.

So. Fancy. Harry Grebshaw had come forward. And this little bugger didn't half waggle those hands when he talked. Funny—didn't match in with the voice. The hands said queer as a cuckoo. The voice said macho. General appearance, half and half. Around these matters the mind of Inspector Rosher flicked as he said, "Do you know what he's been doing for a living?"

"Well"—the dinky hands fluttering again—"he's been with us. A little gardening, general maintenance—things of that nature."

"Here?"

"Why yes. We cannot pay our workers, of course—all our income is expended on the Work—but—I expect you know—Brother Henry had a rather—unfortunate—past history."

"Uh-huh." Good conman once. Fair burglar, but too set in his methods, which tended to lumber him. In a bad patch: dealer in scrap metal. Mostly lead, just off a church roof.

"We suggested—I suggested—to Mrs. Filby-Stratton that she might care to avail herself of his services. The grounds were rather overgrown, there was much to be done. And his—er—misfortunes—would have made it difficult for him to procure employment."

"Who," said Inspector Rosher, "is Mrs. Filby-Stratton?"

The little man widened his eyes, as if in surprise. "Why, the dear lady who owns this house."

"Ah. You don't own it, then?" Filby-Stratton . . . Filby-Stratton. Vaguely familiar.

"Good heavens, no. No. Mrs. Filby-Stratton offered it to us when we needed to consolidate after the mission. People do tend to melt away if there is nowhere for them to intermingle. I live here, of course, your government has been so gracious as to extend my residence. And this week we have our folk-dancing friends from the city. Plenty of rooms, you see, and all the grounds for tents. Would you care to see our shrine?"

"No, thank you."

"It's just in the next room." Flutter, flutter went the hands.

"On the way out, perhaps. Mrs. Filby-Stratton. Does she live here?"

"Oh yes, yes, yes. Sister Gertrude. She's in her bed. She's a very old lady of course, she spends most of her time in bed. Dear soul."

It was very quiet in the room. Not a sound had Rosher heard since he entered the house. Mind you, people might be about out there, you wouldn't hear much through these solid doors and walls. "Is anybody else in the house?" he asked.

"Tonight, no." Out flashed the teeth, up fluttered the hamster hands. "Most unusual. The festival, you see. It won't last, they'll all be back soon. The inner man will make its demands felt. Alas, we are in thrall to our temporal bodies. Although, I suppose, without them there would be no dancing, would there?" Again that rich chuckle rumbled.

"And you don't think," said Rosher, "that Mr. Grebshaw had any particular friends?"

"Not so far as I am aware. I will ask around, if you wish."

"Thank you, sir."

There seemed to be no great point in lingering. Truth to tell, the long spell of duty was beginning to catch up with Mr. Rosher. Behind his eyelids a grittiness was forming; he was feeling that slight sense of unreality which comes as warning that it is time to pull down the shutters. A tired man may miss things. The little man had said he would ask among his flock, and clergymen in general keep faith. He, Rosher, could always come back fresh and bonny in the morning, should a phone call suggest reason. He said, feeling for the black hat, "I'm greatly obliged to you, sir. Perhaps you will be so kind as to ring me at the station in the morning. Detective Inspector Rosher, ask for me personally. They will know where I am if I am not there."

"By all means, suh. Rest assured, if there is anything we can do to help in this dreadful— We all thought highly of poor Brother Henry. Very highly."

"Uh-huh." Rosher had risen to his feet. Four-square he stood, with the hat clasped between hairy hands in front of his barrel chest. "Thank you, sir, for your cooperation."

"Thank *you*, Mr. Russia." The tiny clergyman slipped from the settee. "I shall certainly speak to my flock."

Such Americans—and they were few, he had known very few—as had had occasion to address Rosher by name had invariably pronounced it "Russia." Partly by accent. Partly, perhaps, because Russia is always in the forefront of the American mind, and phonetically received by the American ear off the British tongue, the impact is virtually identical. They left the library. In the hall, the inspector said, "Nice house."

"Big," said the Reverend Mitten. "It requires a great deal of cleaning and so on. Fortunately we have willing volunteers. This is our shrine."

He moved aside to one of the heavy oak doors. As he opened it there came a muffled, soft bumping from the staircase.

Both men looked round and upward. Between the banisters they found a very old lady, using one hand to grip them as she bumped herself down from stair to stair on what was undoubtedly a wizened bottom. Not that it was visible; she was well covered by a sugar-pink nightgown.

The rich voice of the Reverend Mitten welled like a mighty Wurlitzer. "Sister Gertrude! What are you doing, dear, what are you doing?" He fled with hands raised in shock toward the stairs.

Mr. Rosher followed, far enough to bring him to the bottom of the flight, where he remained, looking up, because the mannikin had not halted. By now he was bent over, reaching to get the tiny hands under the lady's arms, lifting her to her feet, saying loudly, as one does to old people, half-wits, foreigners, and the deaf: "Oh, you are naughty. Oh, you *are* naughty. What are you doing out of your bed?"

"Sister Edna—I want Sister Edna," the old lady was saying. A thin, cracked, woozy delivery but a fair carrying tone.

"I've *told* you, dear, she's not *here* today, she has had a misfortune. We'll be holding a meeting later for her, I *told* you."

"The voices," the old lady said. And she really was an

39

old lady, whispy-haired, wild-blue-eyed, and never a tooth in her head. All right, so they might have been in a glass by the bedside. They certainly were not in her head. "I can hear the voices."

That organ voice was truly aboom. "Come along, dear—I'll take you back to your bed. We'll say a little prayer together. We sent the voices away—don't you remember? Sister Edna—and you—and me—we prayed about it. Don't you remember?"

"The voices," the old lady chumbled. "I can hear the voices."

"We'll send them away, don't you worry." When the old lady was lifted up, bent though she was, she stood taller than the pastor, who boomed down at Rosher, using exactly the tone and volume he was using to speak to her, "She thinks she hears voices, poor dear."

"Ah," said Rosher.

"If you will excuse me for a moment—come along, dear—come along, there's a dear." He led the old lady upward. She quavered as she went, "Sister Edna. Where is Sister Edna?"

"Sister Edna will see you in the morning—you mustn't upset yourself—very naughty—you mustn't—"

Left alone, Mr. Rosher stood for a moment twiddling his hat. Then, for want of something better to do, he scratched his left buttock and, with delicately extended forefinger, the ten-penny-piece-sized balding that marred the rare perfection of the short back-and-sides. Then he yawned, and widened his eyes against the sticky grittiness. Then he crossed to the open door of the room said to contain a shrine, and looked in.

It was dark in there. Shutters or heavy curtains or something kept out the light. Shutters it would be, most likely. Curtains usually leak sufficiently to indicate the window shapes. There'd be a light switch. He felt beside the door. There was. He clicked it.

The room sprang to life. Big chandelier overhead, all the bulbs glittering. Around the walls, genuine candles in small candelabra, which, of course, did not light up. Nor did those in big silver candlesticks, one on each side of a blue-and-gold gaudy altar set with a crucifix; but above the altar, on the back wall, the pièce de résistance blazed. A great cross, shaped out by light bulbs in yellow, with above it a splendid star, blazing white against a whole nest of cobalt-blue bulbs affixed cheek-by-jowl in a square, presumably to represent the sky. As soon as the switch was pressed, everything blazed at once. Like a bloody fairground, the inspector thought.

Upstairs, the Reverend Edgar P. Mitten had eased the old lady into her bed, saying "Now—we'll take one of our pills, shall we? Yes—I know you've had one. You can have another. No—no—there are no voices. All right—all right—close your eyes—Most Mighty Brother who dwellest in love and perfect harmony, take away the voices, we beseech Thee. There. I'll just see the window is closed. Not that there's anything out there."

He crossed to the heavy curtains, parted them sufficiently to push into greater concealment with his tiny little foot the small cassette player. Closed the curtains again and came back to the bed. "There," he said. "Now we go bye-byes. Nothing to worry about." The old lady closed her eyes and glupped, already more than half asleep.

He turned away and left the room, fumbling for a key ring to lock the door carefully this time before descending the stair, back to where Rosher still stood at the door of the garishly lit room. "Ah," he said. "I see you have been looking at our sanctum sanctorum. Beautiful, is it not?"

41

"Mm," said Rosher.

"It is at its best when all the candles are lit, of course." From outside the house, faintly through thick walls and those two porch doors, came the sound of a motor engine, voices raised in what sounded like song. Tuneless to Mr. Rosher, but he knew that when everybody roared like that, they were singing. The clergyman, beaming, said, "Ah—here they come now." His heels went clickety-clickety-click as his little legs hurried him toward the front doors.

Rosher followed more slowly. By the time he reached the inner door the little man had opened the outer and was standing aside, crying, "Welcome home, my dears— bless you—bless you" as people swarmed in, coming with the laughing two-steps-at-a-time energy of the born again uplifted by active holidaying among their fellow believers. Young, youngish, middle-aged. One or two older figures less ebullient in the background. They were bouncing from a small coach pulled up in the drive, and they all wore colored top hats decked with red ribbons, ruffled shirts under a black-and-gold waistcoat, blue knee breeches or skirt according to sex, and thick white woolen stockings with gilt-studded clog-type footwear. Passing the Reverend Mitten, they returned his blessing and came on with jokes and laughter and song; and the one first to the inner door, a young female, not looking where she was going, cannoned into Inspector Rosher. "Watch it, watch it," he barked.

She steadied herself and looked up at him. "Whoops— sorry," she said, in a pleasant contralto, and hurried on. I know that face, the inspector thought. Don't I?

The Reverend Mitten was addressing him, from two yards away. "These are our friends from the city. Do you wish to speak with them? Not that any of them knew our poor brother. But some of our own people will be joining us for supper."

No. Rosher was tired. He was chucking it in. "No, sir," he said. "I'll be on my way."

People were still passing the little cleric. He said, "Yes—yes—I shall telephone in the morning."

Rosher said, "Thank you, Mr. Mutton. I am greatly obliged. As soon after nine o'clock as you can manage, if you will." He waited while the last body went past, leaving only the driver of the coach. "Good evening." And he stumped away to his car, nodding to the oncoming driver as he passed.

The driver stopped where the Reverend Edgar P. Mitten stood beaming. "Who's that?" he said.

"A bloody policeman," said the Reverend Mitten.

5

Detective Superintendent Grinly had said it before, in less earthy terms at the Chief Constable's morning conference. And the Chief Constable had agreed, there being no gainsaying. He said it again now, when he and Inspector Rosher had come down from paneling and carpet, one floor to coconut matting and his own less opulent room.

He said, "There's simply sod-all to go on. Sod-all."

"Uh-huh," said Mr. Rosher.

"Look at this lot." The superintendent, seated behind his desk, picked up and cast down a pile of small buff paper. "Dogs. A bloody fortune going out already in overtime, what with this bloody festival and all, and I've got half the force strolling about looking at bloody dogs. And finding 'em, that's the trouble. What are we supposed to do with about a hundred and fifty dog owners? We can't fingerprint 'em—they're not charged with anything—we haven't got any worthwhile dabs to match 'em up with, anyway."

"Parade 'em?" said Mr. Rosher. "Get the people who were in the pub to have a look at 'em?"

Something like this was already in the superintendent's mind. Absurd long shot, but when you are the man under the can in a murder case and it bogs down, you cannot say ach, to hell with it, and pass on to other matters at the end of the first day. Or any other day. Utterly ridiculous long shots have been known to pay off. Very, very rarely, but sometimes richly. If they accomplish nothing else, they give the man something he can be seen to be doing, rather than sitting there supporting his carcass on a fattening posterior.

Both these men had enjoyed a good night's sleep in their own good beds. No telephone call came to start them up in the middle of the night, clutching at a staggering heart; and even this does not altogether suit a bogged-down policeman groping for the turn-off button of the alarm clock. It means nothing has happened in the dirty small hours, and that he is as bogged this morning as ever he was.

No doubt Mr. Grinly was feeling the benefit; but a kind of nervous irritability commonly affects ranking policemen at the start of a case, and frustration exacerbates it. His voice contained an element of snap as he said, "Hundred and fifty of the buggers? What are we going to do, march 'em down to Welford's, line 'em up on the escalator? Keep 'em moving, people from the pub on the stairs in between?" Welford's is the town's big department store, it has this escalator. "And we can't order 'em on to any parade, can we? We can only request."

Rosher was bridling a little. He knew the other man's frustration well enough—wasn't sharing it, but then he was not under the ultimate can—could even empathize with it; but snapped at he would not be. And when he put up a thought, it must not be mocked. His hard little eye was harder as he snapped back.

"They usually cooperate if you hint at obstruction."

"If our geezer *was* in the pub he won't, will he? If he's a pro, he'll know his rights."

Actually, it was in the superintendent's mind that such a parade might never need actually take place. Ask all these dog owners to hold themselves available to attend—look more closely at those who demurred. The inspector was turning into Old Blubbergut, barking "What do you want us to do, then? Sit on our arses?"

"Plenty to *do*." Mr Grinly indicated the pile of forms. "Sort this lot out, for a start. Plenty to do, just nothing to get hold of." Through his irritability he looked over at Rosher, sitting squat and grim in one of the visitor's chairs, and thought, Watch it—watch it—you're getting his back up. No point in that. Hard enough to keep him in line when he's on your side. Rile him, he'll be off doing things on his own. Oh, Christ—he's getting his hankie out. And he braced himself.

When the echoes died away, with the dust motes still whirling and the inspector gone through his idiosyncratic routine—a restowing of the grayish handkerchief, a scratch at the little pink balding, a cough—the senior man spoke again, more circumspectly. Lugubrious, but conciliatory.

"This phone call you had from this clergyman before we went up to the Old Man. You say it didn't help."

"That's right." Still an umbrage in the eye, a grim set to the leather-gorilla face. "Said he's asked around. Nobody knew him, never saw him except when they held their meetings or called at the house." All reported before, up in the Chief's office. True to his promise, the Reverend

46

Mitten rang almost before Mr. Rosher had time to hang up the black hat as he arrived in his office at nine o'clock.

"Tell me again about the setup up there."

The inspector regurgitated his piece, spoken already at the conference, telling of the shrine and the appearance of Mrs. Filby-Stratton. He finished, "Funny setup altogether."

"What sort of bloke was he, this Grebshaw?"

"Well—he wasn't barmy. Always seemed normal enough."

"A lot of 'em do until it hits 'em—" The phone on the desk rang. The superintendent picked it up, said yes, held it out toward Rosher. "For you."

Mr. Rosher took the phone, clamped it against an ear and identified himself. Into that ear came the childlike voice.

"Detective Inspector Rosher?" And he had just said that he was. "Oh—good morning. This is Molly Blenkiron. I just thought I'd call to tell you my sister is much better this morning."

"Uh-huh."

"She had a good sleep. I told her what you said about coming back and we'll be here all the morning. We'll be going out this afternoon for the inquest—well, you know that—and there's poor Harry's funeral will have to be seen to; she'll need a black coat and things."

There'd be no funeral yet. Not until well after the inquest. Not until the coroner released the body; which he would not do until the police gave the nod. "Uh-huh," said Rosher.

"Yes. Well—" Clearly, the voice had expected a less monosyllabic response. A little chat, perhaps. It had no way of knowing Mr. Rosher's invariable reaction to umbrage received from a superior. It hesitated; said uncertainly, "We may see you later, then."

"Uh-huh," said Rosher, and handed back the phone, saying in response to Mr. Grinly's inquiring look, "Grebshaw's wife's sister. Says her sister's more amenable this morning."

"Ah," said Mr. Grinly. "You want to go back there?"

The alternative would be paperwork. Bugger that. "Somebody'll have to," grunted Mr. Rosher. "Might as well be me."

"All right. I'll stay and get on with this lot. See you when you get back. Oh—better take somebody with you."

The stiffness in Rosher became stiffer yet. Behind the mild utterance lay not reproof exactly, but definite official reminder that the book is there, as much in the interest of the policeman as of the interviewee. Rosher's career-long tendency to ignore it had clashed him against the rock of authority too many times for counting. It had also led to many clearings of cases, some highly spectacular, some less so. It was this record, and, some said, the present Chief Constable's favor, that had kept him—they said—from the boot, or early retirement on pittance pension.

He knew what they said. He curled a leather lip at it. And he bridled immediately when authority felt it politic to remind him of the existence of the book, even when, as now, he had decided that company, style-cramping and personally unwelcome as it was, would in this case be wise.

"Uh-huh," he said.

"Grab somebody as you go out." Mr. Grinly bent his eyes downward, to the paper. That'll keep him off my back for an hour or two, he thought. Awkward old sod. Good copper once, but every time he gets near a computer the bloody thing blows up.

This was almost literal truth. Personal radios, electric

48

typewriters, video machines, all the modern electronic marvels foisted upon policemen to help in their work did tend to go on the blink jabbed by Rosher's unloving finger, fixed with his baleful eye. It knows, this glittering gadgetry, when it is not loved, and responds as modern children do. It goes delinquent.

He went now down to the ground floor, where compo flooring clacked under the tread of all but the Drugs Squad, who scuff about in filthy sneakers, to his own office, to collect the black hat. On his way he looked into the CID room. "Who's free?" he said.

Some looked up from typewriters, some from trying to decipher what the hell they wrote last night in the little black book, one from stirring into a cup a dose of liver salts in the hope of lifting hangover. Male and female they were, and they all thought, Christ—Old Blubbergut. Not bloody likely. Suddenly they were all very busy, with the exception of a young man making paper darts out of yesterday's *Daily Mail* and floating them about to kill time between now and coffee.

The making and floating of paper darts in a CID room is not forbidden, nor even severely frowned upon unless the senior rank present is in a foul temper; but neither is it classed as official business. Inspector Rosher fixed the young man with his eye and barked, "What're you doing?"

"Ah," the young man answered.

"If you wear a hat, get it."

He was gone. The young man arose, tall and somewhat angular, and his name was Trevor Dennison. Detective Constable Trevor Dennison. Lucky old you, his happier colleagues said as he followed in the inspector's wake. Immediately, because with that shock of hair he did not need a hat. Enjoy yourself, they said; and have a nice day. To which he answered: Bollix.

6

They walked to the late Harry Grebshaw's house. A temporary one-way and no-go system operates in the town center during Festival Week, and to get to Harry's house from the police station one would have to drive outward and about, and thread in again. Rosher drove it yesterday; but yesterday he planned other visits to follow. Today he was free to take his time on a fine August morning, and every copper likes to see what is happening on and around his patch, which dips are about, who of his little bent is eyeing the innocent festive with intent. So Rosher set off, accompanied by the tall, mop-headed young man to whom he said nothing.

When bunting hangs about and baskets of flowers from the lampposts, and there are banners across the main street announcing various festival functions, the town center really does look rather jolly. Architecturally, apart from some vandal work by Woolworth's and Boots the chemist and a couple of multiple tailors in the lee of a foul supermarket, it has inbuilt Merry England appeal, especially on those glad occasions when sunshine and festivity coincide, enabling people to sweat as they dance beaming in the streets amid the crooked half-timber, the deep-bricked Georgian, and the gingerbread Victorian. Only a mad, mad fool would bet upon fine weather for any outdoor gambol in England; but when it does happen, there is nowhere quite like it in the world. Everything looks so green, so blue, so newly washed. As, indeed, it is.

At ten o'clock the air was still cool, and with the pubs not yet open, so that even the most dedicated clock-watchers were in a state of enforced sobriety or still lacing the breakfast coffee in hotels and boardinghouses, all was entirely decorous. The swiveling eye of Inspector Rosher saw no hand slipping into the unguarded back pocket, no suspicious loitering by a known body in close proximity to the lady with the appetizing handbag. It saw only family groups newly freed from bed-and-breakfast, gladly ingesting the bacon, the egg, the fried bread and tinned tomatoes; young hairy men moving purposefully with guitars to busking stations, accompanied by dollies halo-spiked in green and purple or wearing shocks of hay where they should have had hair; a small male child watering a street drain, minuscule tap held delicately by Mum in a kiss-me-sailor hat. No offense being perpetrated, against property or person. You do not count little boys taken short.

The main street, called Bellgate, and the streets and squares around it are conservation area, most of the buildings being listed as especially salubrious. There are small courts among them, and a cul-de-sac alley here and there; and in a few of these stood minibuses and even a small coach or two, permitted to enter the area by nod of the town council provided they arrived before 10:30 A.M.

51

and did not move out before 6:30 P.M. They brought in
from the outlying villages folk teams and the like, those
who combined a country holiday with prancing in the
town streets and who booked these spots well in advance
by private arrangement with landlords, knowing from
past experience that the public car parks would be full to
overflowing. Some said it shouldn't be allowed, but then
some would ban, if they could, anything contributing to
the benefit of anybody.

Inspector Rosher's bandy legs carried him into Bellgate; and halfway along, standing at the entrance to one
of these alleys—they call them wynds, thereabout—the
flicking eye clamped upon the Reverend Edgar P. Mitten,
small but effective in sky-blue cassock and dog collar. The
legs deviated. "Good morning, Mr. Mutton," the inspector said.

The young constable, attention fixed upon a dolly
dressed for dancing who smiled when he smiled, was traveling straight on. Looking round, he found Old Blubbergut gone. He twisted his head about and saw him
mouthing to a miniature clergyman. Gangled swiftly over
as the little fellow said in a most surprising deep voice like
American ball bearings rolling in a good oak barrel, "Ah.
Good morning, Mr. Russia. I telephoned you, only an
hour ago. Oh—you know that, don't you, you took the
call. Yes. Bless you."

"Out to see the sights, sir?"

"Sights? Oh—no. Not exactly. We shall be working.
About our Mighty Brother's business." White-beaming,
he handed the inspector a tract; handed another to the
young constable, now drawn up by Rosher's shoulder. I
AM THE WAY! it said on the front, black above a yellow
cross with lines spraying out from it to suggest radiance.

52

"Uh-huh," said Rosher. "What do you do, stand here all day and hand them out?"

"No, no. No—we dance. *I* don't personally—the team dances. To the glory of our Mighty Brother. It gathers a crowd, you know, and shows the unshriven that we are joyful. Whoever is not dancing gives out our literature, engages people in conversation—"

In Rosher's opinion, anybody who pranced about in poncy gear to the glory of anybody was definitely crank. But he said, "Like the Jehovah's Witnesses."

"Oh no. No no no. Dreadful people. No no. I am waiting for the team to arrive; if they don't hurry, the coach won't be allowed in the street."

Presumably, the coach was left in this alley. "They've time left yet, sir. It's only a quarter past ten."

"Yes, yes, of course." The little man shut the beam right down. Something went out of the world. "Is there any—news—development—in the—er—with regard to Brother Henry?"

"None as yet, sir. We are working on it. Early days as yet. Good morning."

"Good morning, Mr. Russia. Have a nice day. Bless you." And to the young man, the teeth resurrected: "Good morning. Bless you."

"Ah. Yes. And you," said Constable Dennison, and followed as his leader walked away.

Toward the bottom of Bellgate the coach came nosing along, moving slowly to avoid running over sauntering people who stepped from roadway onto sidewalk to let it through. Inspector Rosher, stepping with the rest, saw nobody he recognized in it; and this was not surprising. His view through the windows was fleeting because the vehicle was on the move, and some of the passengers

53

were seated on the far side, where he could not see them at all. Also, tired as he was last night, he had not paid particular attention to the homecoming team. The face he had thought he ought to know was out of his sight. An impression of gay dancing dress—a face or two—a few ribboned top hats and bonnets—and the coach was gone. A step back into the road, a pace or two, and he tapped a wide man on the back, saying abruptly, "Morning, John."

Even Detective Constable Dennison knew who this was, while the man was still turning. The entire police force in any town knows its betting-shop proprietors. The presence in or absence from town of any of the bent can often be confirmed by his popping up or not popping up in a betting shop. Often, a policeman will call to intimate that should so-and-so roll in, a word via the blower would be appreciated. And acknowledging his debt to the force, without whose restraining influence he would undoubtedly be coshed daily on his way to the bank with a satchelful of cash money, the betting-shop man cooperates gladly.

So this was Honest John. John Todder, known as Honest John; but only by self-proclamation. It rococoed on the banner above his blackboard in the days when he was a course bookie, standing on his box and crying fruitily: "'Ereyah! 'Ereyah! Trust yer money to Honest John." Now he turned and discovered Mr. Rosher with no apparent lift of the heart but no apparent pain. He said with a touch of the hoarseness left over from all that shouting in rumbustuous weathers: "Hallo, Mr. Rosher. Ayn seen you arahnd fer a bit."

"I been around, John."

"Yeah. Keeping well, are you? Doing orl right?"

"Fair enough. You?" Rosher rather liked this man. A rogue, perhaps, but a straightforward one. Bent, perhaps, but not where it showed. Actually boxed briefly, in his extreme youth, as a professional; and in Rosher's heart, nobody who belted people with licensed fist for fun or profit could be all bad. So he bared the great beige teeth jovially.

"Can't complain. Business is bleedin' 'orrible, the punters are picking all the bleedin' winners."

"Should be doing all right this week, plenty of people in town."

"Got no bleedin' 'ackers, 'ave they? Stumers, the bleedin' lot of 'em. Ice cream for the nippers, Babycham for the wife, half of bitter and they're skint. Geezer yesterday wanted to lay five pee on a bleedin' five-to-four favorite. I told him not to risk it, in case he needed a crap."

"Did he?"

"Did he what?"

"Risk it."

"Naow. Wife poked 'er 'ead in, said *she* needed a crap."

Mr. Rosher's great teeth were exposed to the very gum, the simian features were all creased up. From the hairy nostrils came a sort of muffled grunting. Bloody hell, thought Constable Dennison, look at Old Blubbergut—the old sod's laughing! And we are moving on.

"Watch how you go then, John."

"Yeah." Grizzled hair grew low on the wide man's brow. He looked like a bookie who didn't need minders. "Keep yer 'and on yer 'alfpenny."

From the bottom of Bellgate, to reach the house where Harry Grebshaw lived you take a bus. Or you go straight on along the street opposite, which takes you away from the town center; make a right, make a left; make another right, a left, a left again, and there you are. Five minutes by bus, ten minutes by foot to the very doorstep; arriving upon which the inspector stretched a finger at the bell, remembered the thing was not working, retracted it into

55

his bunch of hirsute bananas and whacked the door. To it came the late Harry's sister-in-law.

She smiled quite prettily when she saw them. Not that she was exactly pretty, but to give her her due she was rather comely. Plump and comely and clean. She said, "Ah—Detective Rosher—there you are."

"Good morning, madam." No flash of beige, Constable Dennison noticed. The teeth had retired immediately as they were borne away from Honest John and had not reappeared. But the hat came off.

"Come in, won't you?" the lady was saying. "Bring your friend. My sister won't be long, she's upstairs fixing her hair."

The two men stepped inside. She led them, not to the kitchen where Rosher had stood before, but into a neat living room. From the door she warbled toward the stairs. "Edna—Detective Rosher is here." And to them, in the hostess manner: "Do sit down. You'll find the settee quite comfortable."

Inspector Rosher advanced, eyes flicking over the three-piece suite, the sideboard, the curtains, the inevitable television set. Constable Dennison peeled off toward the settee. "Thank you," the inspector said. "I prefer to stand." The constable veered. One stands, we all stand when the one is senior, especially when that senior is noted for a basilisk eye. The lady was batting her lashes at Rosher, opening her red, smiling rosebud for further speech, which checked and switched as her sister came in. "Ah—here she is." Unnecessary remark. They could see that she was.

Mrs. Grebshaw's hair did not look particularly fixed. Perhaps she had abandoned the job half done when her sister warbled up the stairs. Certainly she seemed more tractable today as she said quite pleasantly, "Good morning."

"Good morning, madam," said Rosher, and waited. It was her place to speak again. She did.

"I am sorry I was—offhand yesterday. I was—upset."

"There," said the sister, on a note of smiling triumph. "We can't say fairer than that, can we?"

"Uh-huh," said Rosher.

"You wanted to know about Harry." A softer woman, altogether different from the virago snap-eyed and hostile in her kitchen, walloping away at the gas stove.

"Uh-huh."

"What kind of thing?"

"Who his friends were . . ."

"If you mean his old friends, he gave them all up."

"Did he have any special ones?"

"I never met his friends; I don't know anything about them."

"She means, of course, *those* friends," her smiling sister put in. "Before he was born again."

"Shut up, Molly," said Mrs. Grebshaw. Quite absently. She'd probably been saying it since the plump lady's babyhood. She would have been the thinner, more forceful elder.

"About this—er—born again business—"

"It's not a business." A trace of snap here. The eye kindling.

"Mm. Rrmph. I am surprised that your husband should succumb." He made it sound as if poor Harry went down with a disease; as he himself went down in childhood—the only time in his life he ever was sick, and his old man clumped him for it—with the chicken pox that turned his teeth that arresting shade of beige. He recovered, but the teeth

57

never did. "I believe it happened at the mission last year."

"That's right. Yes. He came forward."

"So I believe. Did you—er—come forward at the same time?"

"I was already born again."

"Personally," her sister said, "I keep an open mind."

"Will you be *quiet,* Molly. I don't see what this has to do with Harry's friends. The Reverend Makepiece Ewart opened me to the glory on the Monday."

"The Reverend who? Oh yes—that fat Yank who stirred 'em all up. Went away."

"Uh-huh. And Harry—he didn't seem the—er—type—"

"There is more joy in heaven, Mr.—er—over one sinner that repenteth . . ." She appeared to lose her way. Finished: "He came forward on the Saturday."

"Mm." Joy? In heaven? Over Harry? It didn't seem very likely. "What was he doing there? I mean—did you take him along?"

"I was instrumental, yes. He came with me from the previous Saturday."

"And—exposure—all the week—that caused it, would you say?" Rosher's less aggressive interlocutory style owed a great deal to many barristers faced in courtrooms, and even more to those seen on telly during gray, lone off-duty hours in his house on the hill.

"Yes. No. Well—the seed was already ripening. We had discussed matters of—faith—ever since we were married."

She didn't speak badly, this lady. Come to that, neither did Harry. It came to Rosher again, how little he knew of Harry's domestic background. He'd known a little once, and he couldn't remember mention of a wife. He asked, "How long ago was that?"

"Close to two years . . ."

58

"Eighteen months," the sister said. "March. Year before last. I remember because it was just after Joan lost Basil."

Joan? thought Constable Dennison. Basil? Who's Joan? Who's Basil? He'd have liked to ask, not only about this, but what, in general, was going on? He gathered it was all to do with Old Blubbergut's murder case; but the man hadn't told him a thing, had addressed not one remark to him ever since they'd set out. He didn't know where he was, he didn't know why, he was only just understanding that the dark bird would be the dead geezer's wife. And he did not intend to ask for enlightenment. When he joined the force as a very nervous rookie, whenever Rosher hove in sight, more seasoned colleagues muttered: If ever you are out with that old bastard, just stand about and keep your mouth shut.

"Uh-huh." The inspector was thinking, just about the time when Harry dropped out of sight. "I believe he was working. Out at Pilbeam House."

"Yes."

"How long?"

"Since we—the Brotherhood—took it over as our place of worship. It needed a lot of work done, the old lady had been living there alone. He was restoring the grounds and so on."

By the look of them, he hadn't broken his back over the job. "Paid?"

She hesitated. Very slightly. "Yes."

"By your—Brotherhood?"

"We have—the Reverend Mitten has—certain funds."

"From America?"

"I don't know, it's nothing to do with me. Donations, I expect. Collections." That edge of snap was back. "I'm not sure that you have any right to ask about personal matters."

59

Oo, the old twat doesn't like being snapped at, does she? thought Constable Dennison. David Attenborough— on telly—with those bloody gorillas. Quite safe, he said, but you must never irritate them. This one was making its barking noise.

"In the case of murder, madam, we ask any questions we feel necessary. I should have thought you would be very anxious to assist us."

"Now, now," said the sister, "let's not start quarreling again."

"Shut *up*, Molly," Mrs. Grebshaw said. Not absently this time.

Rosher spoke again. "His friends. Did he have any special ones, among your people?"

So much of policing is repetition of the same questions over and over again. He'd already asked this of the Reverend Mitten. From Mrs. Grebshaw he received much the same answer.

"No. Not in the way you mean."

"Thank you, madam." An edge of hard sarcasm to it, a shifting of the hat. "I'll take up no more of your time."

"Oh," said the sister. "Going already?" She seemed disappointed. "I'll see you out."

The entire interview had been conducted upright, on the feet. They turned, leaving Mrs. Grebshaw standing there, and went back to the door, where the sister, as Rosher clamped on the hat, said, "Edna doesn't mean to snap, Mr. Rosher. She's always been like that."

Edna. The name rang a bell. Edna. "Does your sister work at Pilbeam House, Mrs.——?

"Blenkiron." The lashes fluttered, as though question and answer established or deepened some welcomed intimacy. She fancies him, Constable Dennison thought. Jesus Christ! And I know Pilbeam House—it's on my old beat. "Molly Blenkiron. Not exactly. I believe she goes in most days. On a purely voluntary basis. She looks after the old lady who owns it. Mrs. Filby-something. Apparently she's very frail. Can hardly get about, I believe."

Old Fanny Filby-Stratton? said the mind of the constable. She's not *that* old. Well—she's old—but spry enough. Used to chat to her—did her own shopping; I carried her bag once. She's not frail. Well, she wasn't eighteen months ago. It was eighteen months since he left the beat for plain clothes.

Rosher was saying, "Do they call her Sister Edna up there?"

"I expect so." (She's knocking on a bit, young Dennison thought, but she's game. If I were Old Blubbergut, I'd get in there. He'll never get a better offer, outside a zoo. Wait till I tell 'em back at the sweatshop). "They call everybody sister, don't they? Or brother."

"Mm. Well—good morning." The hat, newly donned, raised itself slightly.

"You wouldn't care for a cup of coffee?" the lady said hopefully.

"Thank you, no." Down with the hat.

"Good morning, then." Even now, she did not close the door. She stood and watched as they moved away.

Nobody had taken the slightest notice, all the way through, of Constable Dennison. This did not irk him. He was wondering, as he went along the weedy path beside the forbidding Rosher, whether it would attract barking and general savaging if he broke in upon that man's thinking—presumably he was thinking—to say that he knew Pilbeam House well; and Mrs. Filby-Stratton, who was not all that old and had had, as he now recalled, a gardener, a maid, and a handyman who doubled as chauffeur, when he walked the beat. But as soon as they

61

were out through the front gate, the inspector barked, "All right, lad. That'll be all. Make your own way back."

"Oh—right," said Constable Dennison; and he turned on his rubber heel, thinking, sod you, too, you horrible old bastard.

7

The inquest upon Henry Charles Grebshaw was held that afternoon in the courthouse that is one of the glories of the town, as testified to on television by a delightful old prune who minced about for three days with a team in tow, fluting away in praise of its architecture while deploring its supermarkets, as one in a series called *Our Precious Heritage*. Not many people saw it, the whole set clashed with *Coronation Street*. The old prune was so miffed, he died soon after.

Inspector Rosher attended, of course, and spoke a piece. He was, after all, not only discoverer of the corpus but discoverer of it before he knew it was dead. Superintendent Grinly was there, requesting that it be left where it was for the nonce, and for as long as the police might conceivably find a use for it. Mrs. Edna Grebshaw was there in black, her sister Molly in tweed shirt and slub-linen jacket worn with ersatz pearls and a black armband. None of Harry's friends attended, neither old nor new. Not even the Reverend Edgar P. Mitten. The police re quest was granted, a verdict came in of unlawful killing by person or persons unknown, and Harry was left suspended, held back from putrefaction by refrigeration like a cod on a fishmonger's slab.

The one pressman to arrive hardly counted, he being attached only to the local paper. Not even one of their ace reporters, both of whom were out and about covering the festival and a vegetable show at a village called Hutton Fellowes. His normal function was to gather results of all the town and village football and cricket matches on Saturday. Poor Harry. To the very last, a loser. By the ill luck of an afternoon inquest, even, all the press coverage waving him good-bye would be a blurred stamp in stop-press. Perhaps it afforded some consolation to his spirit, if it was still hanging around, to know that they had used his picture in this same paper yesterday.

As they stood side by side on the courthouse steps in the mellowing sunshine, nobody approached Superintendent Grinly and Inspector Rosher. The pressman went his way. The one or two necessary witnesses went theirs. The two ladies descended and walked off, Mrs. Grebshaw not looking at Rosher, her sister beaming back and waggling fingers, crying, "It seems to be our day for meeting, Mr. Rosher." Which was a daft thing to say.

Neither of these men, the lugubrious thin one or the one who looked like a great ape, had any way of knowing that within the hour Mrs. Grebshaw would be straddled naked in missionary position beneath the featherweight plunging and doglike panting of the Reverend Edgar P. Mitten, small but quite handsomely endowed.

8

The two policemen walked together back to the station, which is not far from the courthouse. On most mornings cars buzz to and fro between, but then on most mornings it is raining, or snowing, or dripping with fog, or blowing a gale. On the rare fine day, even as other men, policemen tend to make the most of it. They walk about a bit, if they are able.

If conversation was not free-flowing as they came through the warm, still-festive streets, this was to be expected. Few people, superiors particularly, found conversation with Inspector Rosher easy, especially when he still harbored a little umbrage stemming from what he considered a slight. They had discussed already his reports, written and verbal, relating to his visit to Mrs. Grebshaw; they had agreed that nothing in them did a lot of good, that they were still up a tree. Superintendent Grinly reopened the matter as they walked, but all he got by way of assistance was a grunt here and there and an occasional uh-huh. When they reached the station he went up the stairs alone to his office with definite feelings of relief.

Mr. Rosher went on to his own room. In a matter of minutes his desk phone rang. He picked it up, grunted, and said, "Put him through." A beery hoarseness shouted, "Mr. Rosher? John Todder 'ere."

"Uh-huh," said Mr. Rosher.

"Sumfing I fort you might like to know. This geezer, the one who got knifed. Wait a minute, I got the paper 'ere—Marion—where's last night's paper? Hang on a minute, Mr. Rosher—ta, dear. Yeah—Grebshaw. Harry Grebshaw, they got his picture 'ere—he was a heavy client."

"How do you mean?"

"Well, I mean heavy, doan I? Slung a lot of bread in. The gee-gees."

"What do you call a lot?"

"Well—wouldn't be a lot in Monte Carlo, but it is for a walking client. Up to four hundred. Three-fifty—it's all in the books, if you wanna see 'em."

Mr. Rosher was sitting up and frowning. "How long's this been going on?"

"Abaht nine months."

"Why didn't you mention it before?" When I saw you this morning, for instance.

"Whaddya mean?"

"His picture was in the paper last night, his death was reported on the wireless, there were bits in the morning papers."

"I ditten know him, did I?"

"Don't you take a look at 'em, your heavy punters?"

"He ditten come 'ere, he used me other shop. I didden know nuffin abaht him until my boy who used to deal wiv 'im rang me this arternoon, seen his picture in the paper."

"Let it hang about a bit, didn't he?"

"Well, he ditten fink it had anyfink to do wiv anyfink. He only works arternoons, for the races. He was ringing in abaht sunnink else, he just happened to mention it. I took a look at the books—course I can't trace it properly, cash punters doan 'ave to give a name, do they, they just fill up the slip. We got one or two heavies, I dunno which entries are him."

"Can't you match it up?"

"Well—yeah—I suppose so. Mean a lot of work."

"Get somebody on to it. I'll come down."

"Orl right. I'll be 'ere all arternoon."

Down went Mr. Rosher's telephone and up he went to see Superintendent Grinly. The superintendent agreed that this indeed could be worth looking at. You want to follow it up? he asked. Mr. Rosher said he might as well. Mr. Grinly did not suggest that he take somebody with him. Honest John was well enough known; if he was volunteering information it was unlikely that he would turn sour.

Within half an hour, Mr. Rosher arrived at the shop just at the bottom of Bellgate. Good business, Honest John was doing. A group of folk singers was yodeling to a button accordion in the cobbled open space outside, but the men in here had no interest whatever in yodeling or, obviously, in button accordions. They stood around in nonfestive raiment, listening intently to commentary on a race in progress, relayed over the interior sound system.

As Rosher's tin ear kept him safe from the full terrible impact of the like of yodeling and button accordions, so his inborn, assiduously cultivated besetting sin of parsimony held him from the equally dangerous lure of gambling. He looked at these men as he made for the door marked OFFICE and thought: stupid bastards.

He had the grace and good sense to knock, and to wait for bidding before he entered. He wasn't here raiding or to unsettle a suspect. John Todder sat squarely at his desk, a cigar sticking out sideways from his face. It was big enough to hang bunting on. He said, "Ah. Mr. Rosher. Come in. I got the books 'ere, last eight months. Not the current one, that's at the other shop. In use. But I got my boy there making a list, and my girl 'ere making another one to cover. Orl right? Wanna drink?"

Rarely during the day did Rosher drink on duty, and then only when somebody else was pushing the boat out or it could be listed among expenses. Here was late afternoon, and a man pushing. "Ah. Don't mind, John," he said. "Don't mind if I do."

"Drop of scotch?" Honest John lifted his voice. "Marion—bring in a glass. And the books." He opened his desk drawer, produced a bottle and one glass. A blond and busty young woman with one of those rumps worked by rotary hipbones appeared from a door, carrying several ledger-type books, a typed list, and a glass. She gave the lot to John, said, "Wasn't much time to do the list properly." "Never mind, dear," said Honest John. "It'll do. Ta."

He waited until she was gone and confided, "Bleeding good worker, that girl. Wooden fink so, wood you, looking at her arse?" He splashed whiskey into the glasses, pushed one over to Rosher with a nod toward a carafe of water, removed the cigar, said cheers, swigged, sighed, smacked his lips, shoved the cigar between them again, and said,

68

"Yers. Now—wot 'ave we?" And he looked at the list.

Rosher also ignored the water. He took a pull at his whiskey and sat with the sparks running down his nose. Honest John pushed a carbon copy of the list across the desk. He picked it up. To the left, serial numbers, not in sequence. To the right, sums of money. Quite large sums. Only five of them, but they certainly totted up. Beyond them names—obviously of horses; who else would be called Fancy Weskit?—together with times and the names of various racetracks.

"There you are," the bookie said. "All cash transactions. Filled in 'is forms, 'anded over the 'alfpennies."

"Bit more than halfpennies, John."

"Yeah—well—" Honest John shrugged, spreading his hands. "You gotta speckerlate to accumerlate."

"Did he?"

"Wassat?"

"Did he accumulate? Did he win?"

"Once."

"Only once?"

"Well—yeah. Doan cop every time, do they? Thank Gawd. The one wiv the star by it. Five to four. Looks like he blued the lot in on the next meeting."

Rosher found the one entry marked with a star. Sure enough, the next showed a corresponding increase in stake money. A loser, at Thirsk. "One in six," he said. "Not much, is it?"

Honest John spread his hands again. "Some 'ave the luck, some don't. You know what the daft bleeders are like. Get schtomped on a loser, they carn wait to get on anuvver trying to win it back. I dunno what's up wiv 'em, I reely don't. More they lose, the more they put on. Remember that silly sod who blew his brains aht in the shop? Done 'is lot, 'e 'ad, 'ouse and all."

Rosher remembered. Two years ago, that was. "And our lad always lobbed it in in cash?"

"We doan take checks, unless it's an account. And if 'e 'ad an account I'd 'ave 'is name and address and everything, wooden I? No—he'd've bin well checked. My boy says he just walked in and out. You wanna word wiv 'im?"

"Yeah."

"I'll get 'im on the blower."

While the other man was dialing, the inspector said, "If he was using bent money he was taking a chance, wasn't he?"

"'Ow do you mean?"

"Just walking into your other shop. He was pretty well known around the town." Among the bent; and the bent are commonly addicted to betting outlets.

"Nao nao," said John. "I ditten mean the Welland Road shop. He used me city branch."

"City branch?" Two shops John had, surely. This one, and the one in Welland Road. Not all that far from Pilbeam House.

"Yeah."

"Ah." It was never Rosher's policy to reveal that there were things he did not know. He sat while the bookie shouted into the phone.

"Alfie? Well—tell 'im I want 'im. Yus—I hope he is bleeding busy. Just get 'im." Waiting, he spoke to Rosher. "Bleeding staff nowadays. Must bleeding argue." Back to the phone. "Alfie? Got the Old Bill 'ere. Inspector Rosher. Nobbled the Avenger, remember? Yeah. He wants a word wiv you. Abaht the geezer in the paper. 'Ang on." Handing the phone to Rosher, he said, "Doan make it too long, they're up to their arses."

70

No need to make it long. The reedy tenor had nothing of significance to fatten the bag. Harry went in, laid down his slip and his bundle of notes and listened to the commentary on the race. Harry went out. That was it. The only time the routine varied was on the occasion when he won, and brought his slip over for paying out. Alfie exchanged pleasantries with him then, but could not remember what was said. Something about his lucky day, and he said about time. Just chat.

What? No, the geezer never seemed nervous or anything. Just—you know—ordinary. You're welcome. Goodbye.

Rosher handed the phone back, swallowed the last of the whiskey, stood up, and said, "Right, John. Much obliged. I can take this sheet with me, can I?"

"Yeah. Want the books?"

"If I need 'em, I'll send somebody round." He resettled the hat, adding casually, "How long is it now since you opened up in the city?"

"Abaht fourteen, fifteen months, ain't it?"

"Long as that? Time flies, don't it? Keep your flies done up."

9

"One thing's obvious," Mr. Grinly said. "He used the city branch instead of one of the town shops to keep it private. Ergo, it was bent money. Question is: Where was he getting it?"

"Uh-huh," said Mr. Rosher.

"You say you've rung his house?"

"Uh-huh." Rosher had, before he came up to see the superintendent. As soon as he arrived back in the station, from his own office. There had been no answer.

"Everybody out," said Grinly.

"The sister said they'd be going shopping."

"Shops'll be closing by now." The super nodded toward his desk telephone. "Want to give it another go?"

Mr. Rosher picked up the phone, dialed, listened for a time, cradled it. "Still out," he said.

"Mm." Grinly stroked his lugubrious nose. Not with the whole hand, as one would to bring a smile to a horse, but using one forefinger. "Mm. And you don't know where he banked?"

"No. He laid it down in cash." Repetition again. Two policemen at work.

"Mm. Trouble is, the banks have been closed for some time. Not much use ringing around, they'll all have gone home. Jammy buggers."

Yes. And furthermore: If Harry had an account fat with bent money, it would not be in his own name. Most likely, not even in this town. To wait until morning before exploring this matter was to embrace unnecessary delay, and to come up probably with nothing after considerable work. The sensible way was obvious. Routine. The super moved the forefinger to the side of his nose, laid a thumb on the other side, and pulled gently. Eased his grip and said, "So we need to have a word with the wife."

"I'll go round there," Rosher said. "If they went shopping, they ought to be back soon."

It made sense. If he stayed here telephoning, he or somebody must call when the phone was finally answered to collect passbooks, check books, any other documentation casting light upon Harry's financial shenanigans. And, of course, policemen prefer not to give advance warning. Arrive suddenly and stand by while papers are being gathered; it cuts down the chance of matter being overlooked or spirited away. Mr. Grinly knew all this. He said, releasing his nose altogether, "Yup. Right. I'll be here when you get back. That—er—that lad. The one who went with you before. Seems a bright youngster."

Broad hint. "Uh-huh," said Mr. Rosher, with no more than small bridling. Truth was, sergeants had been attached to the team by now; and if somebody must go with him, a greenish constable was preferable to a beady-eyed sergeant. Much less trouble, altogether easier to sit upon.

So Detective Constable Dennison was raked out again

73

from the CID room where he was scowling at a type-writer, and stood soon after, as before, on the steps of Harry Grebshaw's house beside Old Blubbergut, black-hatted gorilla and legend in his own lifetime.

They arrived this time in Mr. Rosher's own car, aging but very serviceable and left standing now outside the gate. Mr. Rosher motored down because (a) he'd had enough for today of walking through the bloody town; and (b) because a car is useful for sitting in to wait, should subject be out.

Somebody here was in. Molly Blenkiron. She opened the door and said with what looked like pleasure, "Why—Mr. Rosher—what a nice surprise. Here you are again."

"Good evening, madam." The hat lifted briefly. "I have been trying to contact your sister by telephone."

Why doesn't he just say 'I've been trying to ring'? thought Constable Dennison.

"Was that earlier? I was in the bath. I let it ring, I didn't want to drip on the carpet with no clothes on." And she was batting already. "I wish I'd known."

"Is she in?" The inspector shoved gruffness into the face of pleasure.

"No, I'm afraid she isn't. I left her down in the center of town."

"Ah. Is she likely to be back soon?"

"I really don't know. I believe she was going out to what's-it-called. Where the Brotherhood lives. Did you want to speak to her?"

She certainly had a gift for daft dialogue. He would scarcely have come all this way simply to gaze at her in silence. "That's what I am here for, madam," he said.

"What did you want to see her about?"

"That is a private matter. Between me and your sister."

"No," she said, "what I meant was, if you don't need to

74

actually *see* her, you could come in and talk to her on the telephone. I expect the number's on the pad."

"Ah," he said. "Yes. Thank you."

Once more they stepped into the hall. The lady pointed to a small table. "There it is," she said. "The pad's beside it."

Rosher picked up the pad. It was one of those folding affairs in plastic masquerading as leather, alphabeted down one side for easy reference. He flipped it through. Quite a few numbers and names, written in two different hands, presumably those of Harry and his wife. On the "P" sheet he found Pilbeam House. Before he dialed he handed the pad to Constable Dennison, saying, "Make a list, all these names and numbers."

The constable sprang forward fumbling for his notebook, overreacting in his surprise at being suddenly part of the action.

Mrs. Blenkiron said, "I expect they're only friends' numbers."

"Exactly, madam," the inspector gruffed, thick finger moving from hole to hole.

"Fancy," she said admiringly.

In Pilbeam House the phone rang out. Nobody answered. Where Mrs. Grebshaw was, and the Reverend Mitten, they could not hear it; and old Mrs Filby-Stratton heard nothing very much, these days.

"Perhaps you got a wrong number," the lady suggested. "My phone gets them all the time."

"Grrm." He dialed again. Gave it a full half minute. Put the phone down and said, "You're sure she went there?"

"She said she was. Well, she said if I'm a bit late don't worry, I'd better go and see how the old lady is."

"Hurry up with that list, lad," the inspector said. "We'll go and see her up there."

75

"She'd have answered the phone, wouldn't she?" said Mrs. Blenkiron. "Why don't you wait and have a nice cup of tea? She may be on her way home."

"If she is," the inspector said, "tell her not to go away. I shall be back."

In Pilbeam House not many minutes later, the Reverend Edgar P. Mitten roused himself, lifted his head from between Mrs. Grebshaw's breasts and murmured deeply, with well-concealed loathing, "Are you awake?"

"Mm?" she said, sleepy as a cat replete.

"We ought to be getting up." Naked they were in the bedroom he had made his own; and the reason why his head blinked up from between her breasts was that when their salient parts were positioned for congress, this was as high as it came. His feet were halfway up her shins.

"M-m-m," she went; the soft, elongated sound a woman makes in tender protest when, she released by orgasm from great strain and still drowsed in afterswoon, her lover withdraws and hoickes himself up on his elbows, which in this case were positioned on her ribs. So she added with a jerk, "Aow!"

He plunged again between her breasts, because she shoved the elbows sideways. They do hurt, you know, nobbly little elbows in naked ribs. This time he used his hands. They sank in the soft mammalia. His voice had the timbre of bees in June, in a warmer country than this. "Sorry," he said, giving them a jiggle to please her. "Come on—we have to get up. They'll be home soon."

"Sod 'em," she said.

"Don't be naughty." He rolled off her and slipped from the bed he no longer burned to share with her: small, certainly, but well-knit and sprightly, carrying bravely swinging the paraphernalia of a right good man.

76

She watched him comfortably. Stretched and said, "Oo—that was lovely. You've got more than he ever had. And you use it *much* better. I didn't really need the fix."

She was, he knew, still on the high. It would last for an hour yet. She had been jittery, overwrought when she arrived, coming on, as arranged, directly from the inquest. He had *ordered* her to come, not to speak to anybody. Especially not to the guy who called himself Russia. Not that this Russia seemed more than a dumb copper, a big baboon; but somehow he appeared to rile her. And he, the Reverend Mitten, had learned what she could be like when she was riled and edgy and in need of a fix.

Well, he had given her what she needed, both ways. She was calm enough now, lying there languidly scratching her abdomen and saying, "I love the way the hair grows right up to your belly button."

"I love the way yours don't," he told her, playing the necessary game. One must say something when a fond-foolish woman remarks upon one's pubic growth. Through the door left ajar between this room and the next came a thin, cracked wail.

Mrs. Filby-Stratton was in there, lying in her own bed. "Sister Edna—Sister Edna—" she cried.

Mrs. Grebshaw raised herself on her elbow. "She's woken up. Shall I give her another pill?"

"No, no," said the Reverend Mitten. "We don't want to kill her, for Chrissake. Come on—get up—they're here."

The sound of a motor vehicle coming along the drive filtered in through the window curtains. Had he hurried he would have reached the window and seen it before it stopped; but he had no reason to hurry. All he needed to do was don slacks and shirt and his cassock and he would be ready to greet his returning dancers. So he crossed the room leisurely, hearing the engine cut and doors slam as he twitched aside a drawn curtain and came bolt upright, saying "Jesus!" Because at one side of an aging family sedan stood a tall, gangling young man, and on the other the guy Russia, looking straight at him. The fact that he was doing so owed itself entirely to the policemanly habit of scanning the facade of any apparently deserted building visited, just to see how things look.

"What's the matter?" said Mrs. Grebshaw.

"Get up," the Reverend Mitten said; and then, realizing that in her lingering high she must not appear in front of policemen: "No—stay there." He waggled his fingers at Rosher, baring the excellent teeth, because the bastard had spotted him—he had raised a hand in salute; pointed to the front porch; was now tramping toward it, the young man following.

Had the bastard seen that he was naked?

As a matter of fact, he had not. Mr. Mitten's physical meagerness helped there, in that not much more than his head came higher up the window than the sill. So did the fact that he had not fully opened the curtains. But it rattled the clergyman not to know, and to have him here at all, clearly with some kind of intent. He turned and legged it back toward the bed, saying "My cassock—where's my fuckin' cassock?"

"What is it? What is it?" Mrs. Grebshaw was sitting up by now, a hand covering each breast. Funny how women do that, touched with sudden alarm in an unsanctified bed.

Trouble with people in a high: You cannot predict how they will react to sudden stress. "Nothing, nothing," he said, hopping to get a leg into his little trousers. "Stay here—don't come down—I'll be back in a minute."

Inspector Rosher had not bothered to ring the bell, but he was there. The little clergyman, buttoning his all-concealing cassock over trousers and bare chest, hurried down the stairs, through hall and porch, and found himself face-to-face when he opened the door. Given Rosher's face, this was a situation few relished. "Ah— good evening, sir," boomed Mr. Mitten, smiling widely. "Bless you. To what do I owe this pleasure?"

"Good evening, Mr. Mutton."

"Mitten," beamed the clergyman.

"Rrmph. I understand Mrs. Grebshaw is here."

"Mrs.—no. No. No, she's not here."

"Ah. I was told she was."

"No. No indeed." The beam was very white and very wide.

"Has she been here?"

"No. Not today. I thought she might come up—you know—after the inquest—to seek—comfort. In prayer. With me. But—er—no. No. She didn't arrive."

"You wouldn't have any idea, then, where she might be? She didn't telephone or anything?"

"No. I'm afraid not." From somewhere within came that frail, thin wail, calling for Sister Edna. Mr. Mitten said: "Excuse me a moment." He twisted, keeping his body in the door aperture, and sent his extraordinary voice booming through the house. "Sister Edna is not here, dear, I told you. I'll be with you in a minute." He turned back, saying apologetically, "Our poor lady. She's in her bed, you know. She gets confused. She misses Sister Edna when she is not here."

Something not quite right about you, the inspector was thinking. Not quite easy. And the way you're standing in that doorway—you're not going to ask me in, are you? "Uh-huh," he said. "Well—thank you, sir. If you should see Mrs. Grebshaw this evening, I'll be obliged if you'll

79

ask her to contact me by telephone. At the station. Good evening."

He turned abruptly and led his lad back to the car. Mr. Mitten watched as it made an adequate three-point turn and headed back along the drive. Then he hurried upstairs, going directly to Mrs. Filby-Stratton's room.

The old lady lay tiny in her bed, on her back with a hand over her mouth. The hand belonged to Mrs. Grebshaw, who leaned stark-naked above her. "What are you doing, what are you doing?" the clergyman cried.

Mrs. Grebshaw turned her head with a slight giggle. "She kept calling out," she said. "I've given her another pill, I'm making sure she swallows it."

"For Christ's sake!" he yelled. "Turn her over! Thump her back! You'll kill the silly old cow."

Two hundred yards from the house gate, just short of the big garage, Inspector Rosher stopped the car. Almost for the first time, he addressed Constable Dennison directly. "All right, son—give me that list. You get out here. Get back along there, hide yourself. I want you keeping obbo till I tell you to stop. If Mrs. Grebshaw arrives—on the blower. If she comes out—on the blower. Understood? Move it."

Not a word about how long the lad was liable to be left there, you notice. Not a word about a meal break, no indication as to how he was to get home. Truth, now: The inspector didn't care a bugger about these things. Acting upon the merest stir of a nostril, he was once again seizing the opportunity to shuck the young man from his back.

10

Mr. Rosher was showing umbrage again. Mr. Grinly had received his list with approval and, because it tended to present a simple forename, had British Telecom working even now to match surname and an address to each of the numbers. Mr. Grinly's only expressed reservation concerned the young constable, left standing about. "I don't quite see why you need him there," he said.

"I don't know that I *need* him there," gruffed Rosher. "I *want* him there."

"Yeah—but why?"

Rosher would not say: to get rid of him. On the way back to the station he had stopped to telephone in that list; he had called yet again at Harry's house, to be told by the fluttering Mrs. Blenkiron that her sister had not yet come home; he had treated his expense account to a rock bun and a cup of tea, entering it priced as a full meal, all in happy isolation. What he actually did say was at least partly true.

"A hunch. I've got this feeling she was in there."

Hunches are not too highly regarded in police circles. Plod is what produces the result. Nevertheless, no copper poo-poohs entirely the hunch, when it comes to a seasoned senior man. So Mr. Grinly said, "Yeah. But why?"

"Little bugger was jumpy."

"Yeah, but we're not investigating him."

"We're investigating Harry's money. That means we need to get hold of her. She told her sister she was going there."

"Perhaps she changed her mind, went for a walk."

"All this time?" It was, by now, quite late in the evening.

"She's probably upset. I mean, she'd just been to an inquest on her husband. Perhaps she called in there, went for a walk after."

"He said he hadn't seen her."

"It's the overtime I'm thinking about." Mr. Grinly tuned his voice to a conciliatory tone. He saw the umbrage in Rosher's eye, and he was thinking, Why *must* I be lumbered with the old sod? "We've been bashing it a bit lately, what with the festival and all. The Old Man's asked us to try to keep it down."

"Half the bloody force is on overtime."

True, with a murder case and subsequent hunt for a black dog added to the festival. Rosher himself was working overtime. So was the superintendent.

"That," said Mr. Grinly with a touch of asperity, "is no reason for putting the other half on."

"Couple of hours for one more isn't going to make much difference."

"Many a mickle," the super said. "I think we'd better have him in. It's not as though he's there for any solid reason—" So what do I put in the book? The phone inter-

82

rupted him. He picked it up and said, "Yes. Yes, he's here. Hang on."

Mr. Rosher received the phone. "Yes? Speaking. Uh-huh. Uh-huh." Longish silence. "Uh-huh." More silence. "Uh-huh. Right. Make your way back." He handed the instrument over, totally impassive but with a small gleam in his eye. "My lad," he said. "Mrs. Grebshaw left five minutes ago. In a car. Driven by a young man. Headed the other way, into the country."

When the Reverend Edgar P. Mitten saw what Mrs. Grebshaw was doing, he cried in a loud voice, "For Christ's sake! Turn her over! Thump her back! You'll kill the silly old cow." He then acted upon his own command, because Mrs. Grebshaw was simply standing there, looking at him with mouth slightly open in surprise. He had never shouted at her before.

He came with a rush to the far side of the old lady's small but very elegant bed; and here is an illustration of the dangers implicit in working with people when they are high.

Mrs. Grebshaw had automatically straightened when he shouted. Now she bent over again to peer at the old lady, just as he bent to grasp the wasted body by the arms. Their heads tocked like billiard balls. "Oo Christ!" he said. "Oo Jesus!" And blinking against the rush of tears that comes when the head is sharply tocked, he pulled back the bedclothes, turned the unresisting Mrs. Filby-Stratton onto her stomach, and began to thump.

Nothing came out of her. She showed no interest. "Get hold of her other ankle," he cried, leaping onto the bed. "Turn her upside-down."

His leap onto the bed was sponsored by good reasoning. He was too small to lift the ankle so long as he stood on the Axminster. Now he bent, and, uncertainly perched on the yielding surface, pitched forward onto his face across the old lady's legs. Struggling up, he cried, "Grab the other one—grab the other one!" and seized the near-side ankle. Mrs. Grebshaw did as she was told. They lifted until Mrs. Filby-Stratton was more or less upside down and being jiggled.

Still no little white pill appeared. A good deal of the old lady did, but no pill. "You daft cow," the clergyman hooted, "you've killed her! You stupid cow, you've killed her."

Mrs. Grebshaw began to weep, and she wept loudly; not, indeed, in grief for the old lady, not in remorse, but because he had turned on her and she, in her dwindling high and her besotted state, was not in condition for it. The high itself is unpredictable in its pattern, but the coming down is an emotional mine field, dangerously unstable; and women, anyway, are liable to hysterics, shouted at suddenly and for the first time by a lover whose voice, in its normal tone, alone is a sexual caress. So Mrs. Grebshaw dropped the old lady's ankle and began to cry loudly.

"Shut up! Shut up! Shut up!" cried Mr. Mitten, clutching at a body that was straddling and suddenly unmanageable. What with one thing and another, he had no time to consider the feelings of others. "What are you doing? Grab hold, grab hold!"

"You shouted at me," she wailed.

"Never mind that!" he hooted again. "Grab her!"

"Don't shout at me!" she yelled back, in fuddled shock rather than in anger. "You killed my husband." Through the window came the sound of an engine approaching along the drive and the bray of voices, singing. Among gloomy rhododendrons down by the gate, the only place handy from which he could keep obbo—on the opposite side of the road were open fields—young Constable Dennison noted in his book the arrival home of the dancing party, with the time beside it.

The Reverend Mitten stiffened, letting go of the old lady, who sagged and lay quietly. "Quick—quick," he said. "Get your clothes on."

"You shouted at me," she wailed.

He was by no means inexperienced in the handling of people coming down from a high. He managed to soften his voice into its caressing richness, even to glimmer the teeth at her. "I'm sorry, sweetheart," he said. "I didn't mean it. Come on—" He took her arm. "You go into the other room, get your clothes on. They're home—can you hear them? They mustn't find us like this, now must they."

"You mustn't shout at me." His soft tone was working. She spoke with only a pout.

He was leading her to the connecting door between this and his adoptive bedroom, where her clothes lay as she had dropped them, richly murmuring. "I won't do it again," he soothed. "Now you be my good girl, go put your clothes on."

"I love you," she said tremulously.

"I love you, too." That was difficult. He shooed her through the door. As soon as she was in, he rushed back through the old lady's room onto the landing, to lock his bedroom door. Took him three tries to find the right key from the bunch carried in his cassock pocket.

The coach had stopped outside. The dancers would be leaping from it, those with a leap still in them. Those with no leaping left would follow more soberly. Some would run, skip, chortle, walk round the side of the house to the row of tents, erected in the one-time kitchen garden; but others, on supper duty in the kitchen or billeted in the house itself, would make straight for the porch, expecting to find him there waiting to admit and greet them. He had handed out no keys. Not likely.

He hurried back into the old lady's room. Looked at her. Thought about mouth-to-mouth resuscitation. But she was breathing, quite stertorously now. And mouth-to-mouth resuscitation takes time.

He must get down. They'd thunder at the door, they'd find a way in—the back door, a window. People do these things.

He couldn't have them find him here, glued lip-to-lip with this old lady and with that daft cow liable to waltz back stark-naked or hammer on the connecting door if he locked it. He'd have to open it under their very eyes. The effect would be equally dramatic.

They'd come up, sure enough, if he wasn't downstairs. Of course they would. He'd have to go down. Pausing only to wring his little hands, he hurried from the room. And this one, too, he locked, as the first jangle rang loud and startling from the doorbell. There were people still singing.

They beamed upon him when he opened the door, trooping past as he stood with the white teeth bared to the balmy air, booming, "Bless you, Brother, bless you, Sister . . ." "Bless you, Brother," they said in return, with minor variations; and they clacked over the hall, some going directly to the kitchen to scrub vegetables or whack at the steak with a wooden hammer, others to the big downstairs drawing room with sleeping bags neatly rolled and stacked against the wall. He had put nobody upstairs.

He listened for as little time as he could to an account of the day they had danced through, standing in the kitchen and refusing a cup of tea. "I can't drink tea like you British do," he said. Stock joke at which they all laughed, being loving brethren in God. We can soon make coffee, a sister said. He refused coffee, too. He had to get back upstairs. He listened to the rattle of their collecting boxes as they were shaken at his ear, he agreed that indeed they appeared to have reaped a goodly harvest. Five long minutes passed before he could move out without danger of comment, and when he did he had to force his little legs not to set him at the stairs and gallop him up like a frantic garden gnome.

All that long, long time in the kitchen he had expected at any moment that Mrs. Grebshaw, finding herself locked in, would start to pound on the door. Pounding would not, perhaps, carry to the kitchen; but somebody might well be in the hall, traveling from dormitory room to kitchen or vice versa. And if she took to screaming— that would carry. Women in general have shattering screams.

He unlocked the door to Mrs. Filby-Stratton's room and entered in dread of what he would find. He should have locked the inner, connecting door. He had not been thinking clearly. Suppose the daft bat had come back in— fed the old lady yet another pill . . .

Matters were better than he had feared. Mrs. Filby-Stratton was alone, lying just as he left her. The snoring was gone and she appeared quite peaceful, her breathing light but regular, with little puffs. She did not seem to be dying, she had a pulse. Please God she would sleep the night away and be quite all right in the morning.

He adjusted her nightdress, arranged her more neatly with her head on the pillows, and tugged the bedclothes to re-cover her. Then he went into the next room.

Mrs. Grebshaw naked was very much prettier than you

would have expected. Dressed, she became somewhat drab. She was dressed now, sitting in the tub chair by the window.

He said cautiously, "Are you all right?"

"Yes," she said. Seemed much less elevated. As she should be, of course, by now.

He did not tell her the police had called seeking her, it could have set her going again. He wanted her away—out of the house—quietly. While they were all crowding into the kitchen downstairs, singing their sodding hymns and clattering among the teacups and the scent of cooking steak. He must get her home.

Suppose the police called there? And they probably would.

Have her driven about a bit, until the last sign of instability was gone from her. She'd be all right once she was steady—he'd tell her not, not, NOT to tell them she had been here. Not, not, NOT, on any account. As she valued life and liberty.

"Feeling better?"

"I feel awful," she said. "Hold me. Hold me."

He put his shrinking arms around her. Sitting, she could lay her head on his chest. He stroked her hair—it always lulled her—he spoke very gently, in that deep, womb-quivering voice.

"You must go home now. Your sister will be wondering where you are."

"Yes, darling," she murmured. The stroking, the voice were taking effect.

"When you get there, go to bed. Don't tell *anybody* you were here."

"My sister—"

"No. Not even your sister."

"I told her I was coming."

"Oh." Oh, you daft cow. "Tell her—you changed your mind—you were upset—you went for a walk. In the country. Listen—you must not tell *anybody* you came here. You understand?"

"Yes. Yes, darling." She was getting the sleepy look.

He hoped she did. You cannot be absolutely certain what is penetrating into the mind still hazed from a trip. He wished to God, at this moment, that he had never started her on it, but it seemed a good idea at the time.

"Now—you sit here quietly," he said. "Don't move. I'll have Tony run you home. Into the country first, for a little fresh air—"

"I don't want a little fresh air—I want to be with you—"

"Trust me?" he said. "Will you trust me?"

"I love you." She raised her lips, to be kissed.

"I love you, too." He kissed her. Not for long, but not breaking away so soon as to invite protest. He eased his arms free. "Now—stay here. I'll get Tony organized."

She remained as she was, sitting quietly, while he hurried away, using the inner door into Mrs. Filby-Stratton's room so that he did not provoke reaction by unlocking this room door and relocking it behind him; as he must, not wanting to have her ambling out, probably making her way down to where the merriment was taking place in the kitchen. He couldn't risk that. She might spray darlings at him when he came for her—she might turn stroppy, refusing to leave—general merriment might set her singing and dancing—or she might sink down in tears. Who could tell?

He checked the old lady on his way through. No fresh problem, she was quite solidly with us. Locking this door again, he trotted down the stairs, out through the porch to dodge the kitchen and round the side of the house to where the tents stood. Several cars were parked neatly nearby, property of dancing people from the city Brotherhood who were living here for the week, using the coach to and from town because the company, the singing together, the communal sharing and baring of souls were the major joy of the holiday.

The area showed no sign of life, but as he approached the end tent and reached for the flap, a deep baying came from within, overriding the singing and bursts of laughter floating out from the kitchen. He withdrew his hand hurriedly as a male voice said, "Quiet, Herman. Quiet"; and as the baying died to a malevolent rumble: "All right— you can come in."

He pushed aside the flap and entered, an eye fixed on the black Doberman pinscher that stood braced and rumbling with deep purple lips drawn back over too many teeth. With it were a good-looking young man, lying with his hands behind his head on a sleeping-bag bed; and a pretty girl, bent over a second bag-bed, fumbling for something in a rucksack. Both wore the folk-dance costume. The young man said, "Wop ho, Rev. Don't worry— he's not going to hurt you."

"Are you busy?" the Reverend Mitten asked. The dog lifted his rumble a major third.

"Not particularly. Why? Shut *up*, Herman." The dog subsided. "Lie down. Lie *down,* you silly bastard." The dog—for it was he who was addressed, not the Reverend Mitten—lay down, dropped his head onto outstretched front paws big as Sunday muffins, hating the intruder with his green eyes.

"Mrs. Grebshaw—she's in the house—in a—an unstable condition—"

"Been at the needle, has she?" the young man said.

"I want her out."

"If it's another elimination job, we need instructions from London."

"No, no, no," said the Reverend Mitten, flapping the little hands. "I just want her taken into the country. Walk her around for a while until you're sure she's all right. Then run her home."

"Why don't you do it?"

"I had the bloody things this morning," said the girl, the contents of the rucksack strewn around her. "I can't have lost them." She did not say what.

"You," the young man said, grinning with obvious affection, "you'd lose your fanny if it wasn't fastened on."

"Bollix," said the pretty girl.

"I can't take her," the Reverend Mitten said. "I have to stay here—you know that—I have to conduct the evening service—they'll all start asking questions if I'm—we can't afford—"

"All right." The lad switched his grin to the little clergyman, obviously enjoying his wary watching of the dog, his general unease. "I'll take her. When?"

"Now."

"I don't know if I've got enough petrol."

"Then buy some, for Chrissake, buy some!" the Reverend Mitten said, forcibly enough to set the dog rumbling again. He fumbled under his cassock; brought forth folding money; held out sundry notes. "Here—here—"

"Only joking, Rev," the lad said, grinning more widely. "It'll all go down on expenses."

Mr. Mitten fumbled the notes back under his cassock. "Do it now, while they're all in the kitchen; I don't want her stumbling about with them all over the place."

"Is she stumbling, then? Overdone it, have we?" The lad laughed, teasing. "All right—I'll just change out of this gear. Where's my sneakers, bloody feet are killing me. You coming, Jen?"

"No," said the girl. "I want to sew these tights up, if I can find the needles and cotton."

"I'll bring her down to the front door," the Reverend Mitten said, "as soon as I hear the car." He moved out through the tent flap and hurried away.

Changing from his festive gear into jeans and T-shirt, the lad said to the girl, "He's getting in a flap, our Edgar."

"He's right, though," she said. "We don't want her hanging about if she's on a bad trip."

"Yeah, but he shouldn't have stuck it on her, should he? Wouldn't mind betting he's been mounting her all afternoon, gave her a squirt to improve her performance. Overdid it. I don't like that. I don't like working with people who flap."

"He's not really flapping. He's a bit raw, maybe—it was the inquest today. She was a bit upset, probably, needed a fix and it went a bit wrong. Not unusual, is it, when they're under a strain?"

"Yeah. But bugger walking her about, I haven't had my supper. Why not just take her home, let her go straight to bed?"

"She's got her sister staying, hasn't she? You wouldn't want her talking. Nor would I. Nor would he."

"Yup. Ah well—here we go. Save my share of the steak. Bung it in a sandwich."

"Ah," she said triumphantly. "I *knew* they were here. Needles and cotton."

"Where were they?"

"In the cocoa tin."

"In the bloody cocoa tin? Where's the cocoa, then?"

"I don't know, I wasn't looking for cocoa."

"Bloody hell," he said in comic hopelessness. "Come

here, for Christ's sake. Give me a dirty big kiss before I go."

Down among the evergreens five minutes later, Constable Dennison saw a car appear from round the side of the house. A good car. A young man's car, rakish and sleek. He saw it pull up by the front porch, he saw the house door open and Mrs. Grebshaw come out, escorted by the Reverend Edgar P. Mitten. He watched as the Reverend Mitten took her by the elbow to steer her to the car, he saw her folded in. He drew back into the bushes as the car started, down the drive and past him, turning left onto the road. Away from the town. He made a note of the number and make, adding the time while the little clergyman stood to see it go and turned back into the house.

When he was gone, the constable crept in cover to the gate, slipped through and set off to find a telephone. There was a booth, if memory served, by the garage. He'd tried already to contact the station via his walkie-talkie. No joy. Given flat land, he could have done it; but not with hills and all the houses in between.

11

When Inspector Rosher had reported the bare outline of what his obbokeeping lad told him, he sat back and looked at Superintendent Grinly with an irrepressible small gleam of triumph in his eye. The super said, "Ah. Interesting. Did he see her arrive?"

"No. Unless she was in the coach."

"Coach?"

"The dancing people. They came in, traveling from town in their coach. The lad says he didn't see her among them."

"Where was he?"

"In the bushes. Down by the gate."

"He'd have been keeping his head in then."

The implication was clear. Part of a super's job is to subject every particle of information to the powerful searchlight of his mind. Not every super has one, but they do their best. The lad would not necessarily, Mr. Grinly was saying, have been able to study every mortal soul trotting between coach and house. Briefly, Mr. Rosher replied. "They were all in those costumes they wear. She wouldn't have been."

"Why not?"

"She'd been to Harry's inquest."

"So? She might have changed, gone dancing to take her mind off it. Women love it, don't they, dancing? They do that sort of thing, it quietens 'em down."

"Where'd she change? She didn't go home, the clergyman reckons she didn't go to the house."

"Oh Christ, come on—" Mr. Grinly's tiredness was beginning to show "—in the coach, why not?"

"Hrrm," said Mr. Rosher, who in the teeth of Mr. Grinly's irritability did not intend to be convinced. "Suggest we put a call out, have the patrols in that area look out for the car, see where they go. Registration number C405 STJ." From long practice, he carried such numbers in his head.

"What for? We've got nothing on her—she's just the widow of a geezer who's been murdered. We've got enough to do working on that. If she wants to dance in the bloody streets, let her dance, so long as she's decently covered."

"The clergyman said she wasn't there—"

"Probably she wasn't. If she knew where they'd be dancing, she could have joined them there, traveled back with 'em in the coach."

British policemen do not in general shout and rave at each other as, if television series are to be believed, do their American counterparts. But they can, and often do, mutually abrade. The tapping of Mr. Grinly's fingers on his desk, the stiff look to Rosher's face, the uprightness of his body in the visitors' chair showed that this was being done. As did the barking tone when he said, "I would suggest that we get hold of her tonight. Bang her a bit. Before she has a chance to vanish Harry's papers."

"How the hell are we going to bang her? We've got nothing to hold her on, we can't arrest her. She's free to go where she likes. If she wants to go into the country— all right, who's stopping her? And if she wants to vanish Harry's papers—she's had plenty of time to do that already. Assuming that she *does* want to. Which is assuming that she knows about whatever he was up to. That she's bent."

Anger always, but *always,* went to Rosher's tongue. The slightest whiff of what the hairy nostril deemed fish could translate itself, should the nostril be pooh-poohed, into a great, reeking halibut. He barked, "No doubt she is bent. I reckon they're all bent."

"Who?" said Grinly. "Who's all bent?"

"Her. And the bloody clergyman. All that lot. Up at the house."

A pause. Then Mr. Grinly said, "Christ. Something new is added. Perhaps we ought to go up there and nick the sodding lot."

From the balling of Mr. Rosher's fist he could have been about to unleash the Mighty Hammer, that dreadful ball of hairy bananas that stretched, in its heyday, many a great big policeman twitching in his little shorts on the canvas, many a malefactor supine in many a gutter. "I'll thank you not to take the piss," he said, half-risen from his chair.

Mr. Grinly drew back. Not physically; few policemen flinch from threat of bodily attack. He drew back mentally, knowing that he had, in fact, gone too far. This was Rosher. "Cool it," he said. "Sorry. Bit tired." He rubbed his eyes, for the sake of emphasis. And he was tired. Changing over from night shifts to days that spread on into nights upsets the metabolism. "If you have reason to think they're all bent, you'd better lay it out for me."

Rosher had no valid reason. He had to agree, Mrs. Grebshaw might well have arrived by the coach unseen by Constable Dennison who, being young, was not to be implicitly relied upon, anyway. Keeping obbo is an art. Doing it from bushes, leaves and branches can get in the way. The lad might not have thought of breaking back a few twigs, to give uninterrupted view. As before Rosher's very eyes policemen became more and more absurdly infantile, so fewer and fewer were worth a toss. But he was never the man to retract when ire was upon him, or even to moderate.

He said, "Stunt religions. They're all bloody bent."

No sensible man can answer so sweeping an expression of animosity—directed not toward the activity condemned, but at himself. Mr. Grinly backed a little more. "Maybe. Maybe. But not in any way that concerns us. Our job's a murder inquiry. I suggest we break this up. Nothing we can do here. Go home, get a little kip."

"What about the woman?" Rosher demanded.

"What about her?"

"Aren't we going after her tonight?"

"Leave her till morning. Even if we get Harry's gear, we can't do anything until the morning." And people do not, Mr. Grinly was saying without needing to say, like policemen knocking on the door at night. His private mind was adding, especially policemen such as you, in this mood, arriving like an enraged gorilla ready to rend at the slightest hint of objection.

Rosher stood up. Surely a touch of red showed in the

glittering eye? He said, "Right. If that's how you want it. Give her time to make a bonfire."

"If she's making a bonfire," Mr. Grinly said wearily, "she did it long ago." Odd mixture of tenses, but he knew what he meant. So did Rosher.

"You're the boss."

Oh, for Christ's sake, thought Mr. Grinly, the stupid old sod's impossible. They should have got rid of him when he squeezed that old bag's tits. He said, "Yes, I'm the boss. Now let's all go home. Good night's sleep and we'll all feel better."

The inspector turned and left, with a grunt to serve as good night. I *would* like to have him off my back, Charlie Grinly thought. Trouble is, the Old Man wouldn't go along with it. He thinks the sun shines out of his rectum.

Not true, of course. It was, however, true that the Chief Constable approved Rosher, even indulged him, as a man must approve and indulge the erstwhile hapless whom he has picked up, dusted down, and restored to full pension rights; or confess, if only in his heart, that it was a mistake to do so.

From the look of Mr. Rosher as he flung out of Mr. Grinly's office and away down the stairs, further indulgence might soon be called for. It must be remembered that he, too, had been working a long day. He, too, was tired, although tiredness rarely showed on him.

Now he went down the stairs with brows drawn over glittering eyes, all the leathery seams grim in the simian face. When anger was upon him, so that he swung along, the posterior—which he wore without realizing it—rather jutting as the result of pulling in the belly, originally to disguise the little pot fastened on him by the fat wife's wonderful cookery, stuck out more than ever. The arms, in angry forward motion, tend to swing. Long arms, in

98

Rosher's case. As he went through the reception area, knuckles not far above his bandy knees and ape face set, a Michael Patrick O'Hara, confirmed toper hauled in yet again on a drunk and disorderly, staggered against his supporting copper and breathed: Holy Mother of God!

When he reached his room, the inspector picked up his phone and dialed. It was Mrs. Blenkiron who answered. "Your sister," he barked. "Is she home yet?"

Immediately, Mrs. Blenkiron went more girlish. "Oh," she said. "Mr. Rosher, is that you?"

"It is, madam."

Even yet, after years of women's lib, there are women who thrill when barked at by a powerful male. Closer acquaintance may turn her off, but in the initial fancying stage it makes waves in her. "I'm afraid she's not," the lady said, fluting-sweet. "I'm the only one here. I was watching the telly."

"Kindly notify me when she returns," he barked. "Here at the station." The duty operator would see to it, as routine, that the call was passed on to him at home.

"My word," she said, "you work all hours, don't you?"

"We do, madam. We do."

"If you'd like to come and wait here, you'd be very welcome—"

But Rosher was gone. Had slammed the phone down and was reaching for the black hat, hanging on the peg behind the door.

No call came that night. He went home and slept badly; not because he was wondering what on earth could have happened to Mrs. Grebshaw, and certainly not on account of collision with Superintendent Charlie Grinly. It was his firmly held belief that if collision occurred between himself and any other man, the other man was a twat. Shielded thus against the self-doubt that leads to tossing and turning, so long as he stood to lose nothing by it, collision never interfered with his sleep. What held him sweating and swearing between bouts of colorful dreaming was, very simply, a new stirring of the antennae brought about by his actually voicing the opinion that the Pilbeam House setup was bent.

To call him an atheist would be to exaggerate his interest. Truth is, he never gave a thought to religious matters. He lived entirely, by nature and training, in the here and now, seeing all humanity as bent or potentially bent; and with humanity he lumped religion. All bent, from the Pope down. And none more so than your stunt-men.

Given this outlook, it follows naturally that one out-of-kink happening—two, if you count the Reverend Mitten's apparent unease when he, Rosher, called—should set the antennae waggling; faintly at first, more definitely once he had spoken.

It was true, what Grinly said: Their business was to pursue a murder inquiry, not to go chasing after side issues. But it was the Pilbeam House setup that plagued him during the night. And Harry had been part of it. And Harry, it seemed, had suddenly found a lot of money with which to play the horses.

And no call to say that Harry's wife was home.

So: Had she scarpered? Or something? With a young geezer? Was that car bound for far away?

Or did it come back? With her in it? And here a faint sense of having done something wrong touched him. He shouldn't have called young Wot'sname in—he should have left him there, bugger the overtime. Sent somebody from late shift to relieve him, gone out himself instead of wasting time arguing with Grinly.

Officially, of course, he couldn't. No grounds for keeping an officer tied up on overtime, for tying up a relief man who should have been deployed elsewhere. Nevertheless, it irked him that he had not done so. If it did turn out that the house was bent—and he'd bloody bet it was—he would have been justified.

Yes, yes, yes. But Grinly wouldn't countenance it. Twat.

He climbed out from the rumpled bedclothes early. Took a bath, stumped about his dusty, silent house in dressing gown and slippers, frying bacon, cursing when the egg yolk broke, cutting thick slabs of bread and cursing again because he had run out of margarine to spread it with, brewing black and wicked tea. Consumed the lot, even washed up, and was climbing into the durable suit by six-thirty. Fine morning again; and he'd go to Harry's house. Now. Well—as soon as he'd had another mug of tea.

Why not? A good rule always: Bang people with surprise. Don't ring—call. In person. You learn more from faces than from voices. Also, by going now, he could bend the book.

Nothing had happened re Harry during the night. He, Rosher, should not, of course, stray beyond reach of a telephone without letting the station know where he was going, this is the rule when a man is part of a murder inquiry. So—

He would not ring the station. Phone calls and their contents are logged, with time of origin. Bending the book, he preferred not to have matter in black and white. He would call at the station on his way, just to ensure that everything was quiet. Casual conversations are not recorded. Nobody would comment upon his being about early, the comings and goings of CID officers conform to no set pattern and he makes no account of them.

He'd call in, let the desk sergeant believe he was going

for breakfast in the canteen upstairs. Up at the front, down at the back and out through the unobserved CID door. He'd be there and back by nine, with half an hour in hand before the Old Man's morning murder conference, with coffee in the tiny cups and a couple of Garibaldi biscuits.

All of which subterfuge might appear unnecessary, since Mr. Grinly would be authorizing a visit to Mrs. Grebshaw as first activity. But Mr. Grinly might decide to come with him, thus getting in the way. Or he might send somebody else. And he, Mr. Rosher, was still umbrageous toward Mr. Grinly. In the morning, he had said. Leave her until the morning. Well, it was the bloody morning. And a start at ten o'clock, after the Old Man's conference, was too late. People had their faces fixed by then. Not for the fun of it do police raids happen at dawn.

He was on Mrs. Grebshaw's doorstep soon after seven, his car left prominent outside the front gate because it often proves a rattler, the interviewed's concern over what the neighbors will think about a police visit out of normal working hours. The policeman was in plain clothes, and his car unmarked; but they know, you know. They know.

Mrs. Blenkiron answered his knock and looked immediately disconcerted. "Oh," she said, pulling the neck of her dressing gown closer. "I thought it might be the milkman, but it's not. It's you." No smile. And no batting of lashes. No lashes worth batting, they were upstairs on the guest-room bedside cabinet. She looked smaller, younger, more vulnerable without makeup. But no less plump. Some might have preferred it.

Rosher himself might, in the days of his steaming libido; but those days were far behind. "Good morning," he said brusquely. "I assume your sister is here?"

"Well—yes," she said. "She's still in bed."

"She came home last night?"

"Yes. About ten."

"By car?"

"No. Well—I don't think so. She just came in."

The lad Tony had, in fact, had the good sense not to drive up to the house. Dropped her at the end of the street, let her walk the rest.

"I requested that you ring me when she arrived."

"Yes. Well—it was late. And she went straight to bed. She looked very ill. I thought—you know—I thought she'd better be—she'd had enough. I thought you wouldn't want—I thought she needed a good sleep—"

"We all need a good sleep, madam. I myself was up half the night waiting for you to call." A lie. A blatant lie.

She answered with a flash of spirit. "You could have rung again. We were here. She is my sister, you know, her husband's been murdered, she'd been to the inquest and all. And she can't even bury him. Blood's thicker than water."

"It's in view of her husband's murder that we need her cooperation." The bark. The Old Blubbergut bark. And again she reacted with spirit.

"Not when she's ill. Not in the middle of the night, when she's ill. Her place was in bed."

"Ten o'clock is hardly the middle of the night."

"How was I to know how long it would take for you to arrive? When my Arnold had his attack, it was three hours before the ambulance came. And that was 999."

"Arnold?"

"My late husband. Dead on arrival."

"Shall we go in, madam, or would you prefer that I see your sister here?" Because, his face and voice said, see her I shall, never mind your bloody Arnold.

For a second she hesitated; but really, she had no

103

choice. She was not dressed for talking to men on door-steps. Nor, presumably, would her sister be for some time, if she was still in bed. She stood aside, still without the welcoming smile. "Yes," she said, "you'd better come in, we can't stand out here."

He stepped in, only now removing the black hat. His early start meant that his chin shone with the blueness of close shaving. The seams of his face had absorbed as yet no grime, the boxy-toed shoes gleamed with pristine polish. If she, in dishabille at seven in the morning, was not impressed with the image of police alertness at all times, she should have been. But probably she did not think about it. The public generally takes it all for granted. She showed him into the living room, saying, "I'll just slip up and tell her."

Crippled though he was in the libido, enough of it functioned yet for him to notice how her breasts filled the upper front of that dressing gown; and when she turned to leave, that she still had a most definite waist. The region from there down would have done credit to a honeybee. He waited in the living room for some time. Long enough to open the sideboard cupboards, to look in the drawers. Nothing in there but crockery, bits and pieces. Unless the widow had taken them away, Harry did not keep his papers in here. He was standing well away from the sideboard when she returned.

She had taken time enough to tidy her hair, to dab on a little powder and add a touch of lipstick. The dressing robe had been exchanged for a flower-patterned frock. She said with something of her old manner, "I've told her you are here. She should be down directly."

"Thank you," he said; and silence settled awkwardly until she said, "Won't you sit down?"

"Thank you, I prefer to stand."

"Ah. Would you like a cup of tea, while you wait?"

"No, thank you."

"It won't take a minute. We always have a cup, first thing."

"Thank you, no. Did your sister say where she went yesterday?"

"No. Not when she came in. She went straight up. When I asked if she was all right, she said she felt off-color, so I filled her a hot-water bottle."

"What about Pilbeam House? Didn't she say she was going there?"

"Yes. Well—she said she might. After the inquest. But she may not have done, she might have gone for a walk."

"Walk?"

"Or—the pictures, or something. People do funny things when they are upset, don't they? I mean—I expect she just wanted to be on her own for a bit."

Four-square and unyielding he stood; and because he had declined to sit down, neither did she. Through a new awkward silence she stood and dithered, said, "I think I'll just put the kettle on. Are you sure you won't have a cup?"

"Quite sure."

"Ah—well—excuse me—I'll just . . ."

She went out to the kitchen. No sign of Mrs. Grebshaw. When the sister returned, empty-handed, he said brusquely, "Your sister seems to be taking her time."

"Ah. She was still asleep when I went up. She's not at her best in the morning." Delivered with the smile of the hostess. She was rapidly coming back to form. Quite brightly, she said as she left the room again, "I'll give her another call." Which she did from the hall, fluting up the

105

stairs, "Edna! E-e-ednah! Hurry up, dear, Mr. Rosher is getting impatient."

She came back. Another minute passed, and a minute can be a long time spent with a mute gorilla. When Mrs. Grebshaw entered, she did indeed look ill. She made no sound on the carpeted stairs, she came in silence and stood looking at Rosher with hostile eyes burned into a chalk-white face. Mrs. Blenkiron said, beamingly triumphant, "There! Here she is."

"Good morning, madam," said Rosher.

"Good morning." Hostility. She wore a dressing gown over an obvious nightdress, and her body and hands seemed shaky; but eyes and voice were strong enough. "What time do you call this?"

"There is a matter into which we need to inquire urgently. Your husband appears to have been gambling heavily."

"Gambling?" Was that a momentary flash in her eye, a flash quickly hidden? "What gambling?"

"Horses. Large sums of money."

"Money? He never had any money."

"Sit down, Edna," said Mrs. Blenkiron. "Sit down, dear, you look very peaky."

"Be quiet, Molly."

"I take it he had a bank account?"

"Yes. But he wouldn't have had much in it."

"I would be obliged if I can take his check books and statements away with me. Together with any other documents relative to his financial affairs."

"What, now?"

"Now."

"Fancy," said Mrs. Blenkiron.

Her sister said, "I don't think you have the right—"

106

"I am making a request, madam. If you prefer it, I can come back with a squad and a warrant. Search the house."

Mrs. Grebshaw hesitated, said abruptly, "Wait here," and left the room.

Had he been entirely fixed upon this financial aspect, he would have gone with her, whether she liked it or not, but his main interest was in her having visited Pilbeam House. Assuming that she shared something funny with Harry, he knew as well as Mr. Grinly knew that anything she believed should be hidden or destroyed had been dealt with long ago. Any accounts involved would be in false names. The documents would not be here. She would not be making a bonfire now. But she would, at some time, attempt to cash in. Therefore. Don't over-press. Just let her know we are on.

Sure enough, she came back with one checkbook only, and a couple of bank-statement envelopes. "That's all there is," she said.

It was about what he had expected. He put the lot into his inside breast pocket after a glance at the balance. "£150," it said, written in Harry's ballpoint. Presumably it was Harry's. He said, "I'll give you a receipt. The articles will be returned to you." And as he made out the slip, sitting on a hard chair to provide himself with a knee: "I believe you visited Pilbeam House yesterday."

"Me?" she said.

"Uh-huh." His hard little eyes were watching from under the down-bent brow. She looked disconcerted. Momentarily, but definitely.

"No. Not me."

He did not say: I had a man in the bushes, he saw you. It was enough that she denied it. Fish. Therefore: Do not blow the fact that as far back as yesterday you were keeping obbo on the house. He said quite mildly, "I understood you went into the country. In a car."

"Not me. Who said so?"

"Just one of my lads, driving along. Said he thought he saw you."

"Well, he must have been mistaken."

Wariness pulls people together. It's the sudden kick of adrenaline. Changes the entire glucose and lactate content of the blood. Her hands and body no longer trembling, she looked very much better. Alert. There was now no doubt, she would live through the day.

"Uh-huh." He stood up to hand her the receipt. He would shove no further now. He had what he came for, and it was not Harry's checkbook. Without backup in the shape of at least a couple of men keeping obbo at the house, to panic them might well mean that all trace of whatever they were up to was vanished long before any action could be taken. If any action could be taken.

Is it strange, or is it not, that he never once considered that reluctance on her part, and that of the Reverend Mitten, to reveal that she was at the house yesterday could be due to the fact that he was knocking her off? He saw her drab look, he saw the little man's daintiness, and never gave the possibility a thought. A woman would have known the power of that deep, rich voice, the pull of maternal instinct and, even, the tempting curiosity regarding the truth of an old saying about little men. The Reverend Mitten knew all about these things. He never had trouble finding women. And in his case, to their comfort and delight, the old saw held very, very true.

"Is that all you want?" asked Mrs. Grebshaw.

"Yes. You'll get them back when we've finished with them."

"I should hope so," Mrs. Blenkiron put in. "She's the next of kin."

"Be quiet, Molly."

"Yes, dear, but you'll need every penny you can get. It cost me three hundred pounds just to bury Arnold; if I hadn't paid into a club—"

"Be *quiet*." Mrs. Grebshaw never seemed to look at her sister when she commanded quiet. Her hostile eye remained fixed now upon the inspector. "You'll be leaving then."

"Yes, madam. I'm leaving." Equal hostility. The bark.

Mrs. Grebshaw made no move, spoke no word of farewell. Mrs. Blenkiron said, resuming her hostess sweetness, "I'll see you out."

Once again, her breasts seemed to inflate as she stood by the open door, reaching out as he pushed past. She bade him good-bye with her normal flutter, less impressive than usual, perhaps, for still lacking the lashes, and stayed to watch him drive away. When she turned back into the house, her sister, looking very shaky again, was already at the telephone.

She did not hear the conversation. She tried, while Mrs. Grebshaw dialed, to linger in the hall; but Mrs. Grebshaw snapped, "Do you mind? This is a private call."

The imputation incensed Mrs. Blenkiron sufficiently to send her into the living room, where she closed the door pointedly behind her; so that all she knew for certain about the call was that her sister made it very hurriedly when Mr. Rosher left, and that she fumbled the dialing, the sick and shaky look back upon her.

12

In the small breast of the Reverend Mitten, the call gave rise to alarm. He, too, was guarded in his speaking because the phone was in the hall and there were dancers about. It was still too early for prancing in the streets. They were at breakfast, or at private prayer in the shrine—gluttons, these; he would preside over a service before they left, as he did every morning and again in the evening when they returned—or passing to and fro. Several times he had to beam while he was speaking. When he hung up he checked the kitchen, and finding the pretty young couple not there, went out to the tents.

That damn dog began to bay the second he touched the flap. He waited while the lad Tony cried, "Shut *up*, Herman. Be *quiet*. Lie down! All right, you can come in."

They lay, he on his back and she with her short-cut head on his shoulder, in two sleeping bags zipped together. Very attractive. The lad smiled brilliantly, having no need of a glass beside the bed in which to keep his teeth. They were almost as white, if not quite so abundant, as Mr. Mitten's own. Not that he had any missing; the Reverend Mitten had more. He said, "Morning, Rev. We were just thinking of having a quickie, set us up for the day."

"Never mind that." The dog growled low as soon as the little man spoke, and was firmly hushed by Tony. "I've just had a call from the Grebshaw woman."

"Yeah? What did she want?"

"The police have called."

"Well, they would."

"This *morning.*"

The handsome eyes showed interest. The girl's head turned as she, too, looked at Mr. Mitten. The lad said, "Already?"

"That's just it. They'd just left. He had. What was he doing, calling so early?"

"Who's he?"

"Name of Russia. He's an inspector, looks like a gorilla. He's the one Harry was fixing to meet. He was here—I told you—and he came yesterday afternoon. I told him she wasn't here. Somebody saw you with her. In the country."

"Who?"

"I don't know—did you pass a patrol car or anything?"

"Not that I remember."

"She told him it wasn't her—she said whoever said it was was mistaken. She says he took Harry's bankbook."

"Shit." Quick-witted if not verbally elegant, the young man knew that large sums going into a workingman's account create interest. He also knew the principle of several accounts under false names, so he said, "He wasn't a mug, was he, your Harry? He wouldn't have shoved it all in under his own name?"

"I don't know what he did with his money," said the

Reverend Mitten. "Nor does she. All she's found is his current account. She can't find anything else."

The lad relaxed, toying with the girl's boy-haircut. "Well, if she can't, I reckon they can't. If he hid it right—"

"This guy—this Russia—says he was gambling heavily—"

"Gambling? Where?"

"I don't know—that's all she said."

"Bloody idiot. How much?"

"She didn't know that either. Just large sums, this Russia said."

"Was he gambling when you took him on?"

"I didn't take him on. London wished 'em on me. They'd spotted the house—London told me to get it—the States must have okayed it—they told me to contact this guy and his wife, work with them—"

Brutally, the young man said, "Did they tell you to start knocking her off?"

The Reverend Mitten's mouth opened slightly. He hadn't known the young couple knew. Sexual liaisonists often believe themselves to be more private than they actually are. "I—never mind that," he said. "She started it."

"You hooked her on the smack."

"She—she was hooked already."

The young man did not say you're a liar on both counts, he did not even look skeptical; but he did not believe. The big organizations do not mess about, they will not use anybody hooked. Too unreliable, and becoming progressively more so. And if somebody—the Reverend Mitten, for instance—finds himself linked with somebody hooked, it is his duty to report it. This Tony had the situation carefully under surveillance, but he knew his job. Now was not the time to rock the boat. So he said, "Well—so long as he buried it deep—if he didn't blue it all in—I don't see any imminent danger. They can't touch her—she's just the grieving widow. So she comes up here. Spiritual comfort—you're her guru, aren't you? And she's Sister Edna, she's been coming here for months, nothing hidden about it."

"Yeah—yeah—but I told the guy she wasn't here yesterday. He's gonna be back."

"So? If they saw us in the country, that's not here, is it?"

"No, but—"

"Listen—you're not a bloody amateur. You're supposed to be an actor, you should be able to handle him. If he calls."

"I don't like it. I don't like him bobbing up all the time—"

"Bound to, isn't he? One of your flock's been killed."

"He shouldn't have been—"

"That's down to you."

"Not like that. Not the way you did it. Not in a crowded pub."

"We had to get him before he saw your Russia."

"Not—you could have—I thought you'd—vanish him. Hide his body—somewhere—so they wouldn't find it—"

"Didn't have time, did we? These things need planning. We had to do it quick, best way we could."

The girl, listening, thought, And you find it more fun, don't you? The almost public execution—the adrenaline charge—the sense of omnipotence—the frenetic sex, the elated coming, the gaiety for days after. That's the appeal of the job.

"It made headline news out of it—why couldn't you do it somewhere quiet—"

"We didn't have time, for Christ's sake. He phoned this Russia, right? She told you, you told London. If we hadn't been in the city, we'd never have got here in time; if she

113

hadn't told us the pub he was meeting your Russia in, we'd never have come up with him. Certainly not before he talked. We'd never even met him; I had to ask if it was him. You consider yourself lucky, little man."

"Yes," said the Reverend Mitten. "Yes, yes, yes." He turned abruptly and left the tent. The dog rumbled. The lad rose to sitting position. Very beautiful, naked and visible to the waist.

He said, "The little sod's running scared. I don't like that. Maybe we ought to ring London, see if we ought to do something about him."

"Trouble is," she said, "they want the house. He's the kingpin there."

"Yeah, I know. But I think we ought to give 'em a buzz. If they say just stick close and watch him—okay. If they say put him down—okay. So long as they're in the picture, we're in the clear. I know what I'd do."

She rose to sit beside him. Even more beautiful, with her sloped and slender shoulders, her pertly nippled breasts. She interspersed her speaking with naughty little flicks with the tip of her tongue into his ear.

"You like killing, don't you?"

He returned question for question. "Don't you?"

"No," she said. "Not all that much. Not like you do. But I love what it does to you after."

He turned to kiss her, teasing the nearest nipple into a sweet loganberry. "You're a randy bitch," he said. "A right little raver."

"I know, I know," she crowed between kisses.

"How about," he said, "that quickie before breakfast?"

Mr. Mitten was by now reentering the house by the front door. His flock was active, shooting about from kitchen to and fro, wherever they were coming from or

114

going to. He bestowed a beam and blessing upon several as he hurried upstairs for the gold-and-purple robe he must don over his cassock to preside at their morning service in the shrine room.

He checked again on old Mrs. Filby-Stratton while he was up there. She had come though the night all right. Still sleeping, but breathing nicely and looking healthier. Thank God for that. She mustn't die jam-packed with drugs.

A few minutes later he was in front of the improvised altar, intoning in his rich, impressive manner, "O Mighty and All-Harmonious Giver, father and mother of our Most Mighty Brother, vouchsafe unto us . . ."

"Amen," they said, and "Hallelujah." Hallelujah. Praise the Lord.

13

Superintendent Grinly had not gone home immediately after Inspector Rosher left him the previous night. He stayed long enough to ring the local paper and arrange with the night editor for a squad-car man to collect prints of their file picture of Harry Grebshaw—the only one known to exist. He had waited on, and when they arrived had sufficient copies made and dispatched to cover all the police stations in the town and the big city ten miles away, to provide a flying start that morning. By the time he arrived for the Chief Constable's conference at nine-thirty, policemen were already calling at all the banks and building societies, asking if any of the staff recognized this man.

Inspector Rosher himself came back to the station with plenty of time in hand before the meeting. When he left Mrs. Grebshaw's doorstep he considered a quick run over to Pilbeam House to challenge the Reverend Mitten there and then with a flat declaration that the lady had been seen leaving; but it might well have made him late. Ab-

116

sence from a Chief's meeting as a result of pursuing unauthorized business is not tolerated, especially when no
contact has been made, and to make contact is to be called
back instanter, with rockets zooming around and spatter-
ing all over the record. The book may be rumpled, but
never torn up.

So back to the station he came, where he did a little bit
of this and a little bit of that—paperwork relating to other
cases, because a detective's in-progress work does not con-
veniently cease when he is lumbered into a murder inquiry—and still had time for two mugs of stygian tea and
a browse through the newspaper while he sank them. A
quick call into the lavatory—the liquid content of canteen
tea, they say, goes right through you (the tannin lingers
forever)—and he arrived in the Chief's office only seconds after Mr. Grinly, who went straight up as soon as he
had parked his hat and smoothed down at the sides such
hair as God had spared him.

Only the two of them were there, to be served by the
Chief himself with coffee they did not want in those cups
which Rosher feared and hated. Fragile wee things, they
were. Bone china. Nobody who once boxed in the heavyweight division can set fur-backed fingers to such without
being distractingly certain the handle will come off, or the
whole bloody thing embarrassingly disintegrate. Large-
pattern policemen prefer a thick clay mug. They lack, in
general, the inborn talent that enables a man to balance
with insouciance a tiny cup and saucer in one hand while
nibbling a Garibaldi biscuit from the other.

"Well, gentlemen," the Chief said when he had them
seated and served. He himself could handle china, in all its
multitudinous forms, with enviable élan. He had a delicately nurtured wife, and her bridge rolls were famous.

117

She certainly could make a bridge roll. "What have we to examine?"

Very little, on the official level. This is why only Mr. Grinly and Mr. Rosher were present. No need for Uniform Branch chief to attend, his men were engaged as routine. No need for Forensic, or any other specialized department. They had performed, reported, and passed along to other work. It took only a minute for Inspector Grinly to fill in most of what the Chief did not already know.

He finished, "We're bogged at the moment. Nothing on the black-dog angle. Things may open up when we find out where he got his money, where he kept it."

"He may not have run an account at all," the Chief said, "if he was into something criminal."

"True," said Grinly. Policemen know very well that the bent element prefers the cash transaction. A sock under the mattress gathers no incriminating paper.

Mr. Rosher spoke, keeping his eyes away from the superintendent. "I went to see Mrs. Grebshaw, sir, before I came in. Collected his checkbook, couple of statements." He reached into his inside pocket, handed over the documents. "That's all he left, she says. As you can see, not much in it."

The Chief, taking the material, glanced at Mr. Grinly, saw the sideways flash of eye, the setting of the lugubrious face. What's that for? he asked himself. Has Rosher preempted him, did he want to report it himself? They're all so touchy, so quick to bridle over matters of rank and protocol. Aloud he said, deliberately addressing the senior man, deliberately putting him back into his rightful position, "Well—he couldn't gamble much with that, could he?"

He had no way of knowing that Rosher had been off

again, proceeding under individual steam; that the inspector had chosen to reveal his movements and material here, rather than to Mr. Grinly earlier—as he could and should have done, by phone if not face-to-face—to avoid certain clash until he had him, the Chief, maneuvered to act as buffer. Nor was Mr. Grinly going to tell him. There are things you do not tell your totem-topper, among them, that a rorty old bugger under your command is going his own way.

So the superintendent said stiffly, "I haven't seen the documents yet, sir. I arrived, you'll remember, before Mr. Rosher came in."

"Yes. Mm." The Chief passed the material on. Mr. Grinly studied the balance marked on the last check stub, glanced briefly at the statements. He said, "Doesn't mean a thing, does it?"

"Unless," said Rosher, "the woman is also bent."

A slight pause. The muscles in Mr. Grinly's face were not loosening. The Chief said, addressing the air between, "Do we have reason to believe she might be?"

Mr. Rosher glanced at Mr. Grinly. He could have it now. The superintendent said, "We had a man keeping obbo at the house, sir. He reported seeing Mrs. Grebshaw leaving in a car driven by a young man. Soon after the—er—vicar—the parson—had stated that she was not there."

"Uh-huh. And we consider, do we, that in some manner this involves her in our murder inquiry?"

Put in this way, it sounded embarrassingly thin. Even Mr. Rosher must have felt that. Certainly, he remained silent. Once again, answer was left to Grinly, who stiffly drew on the pomposity to which policemen and politicians are prone, needing a sudden shield.

"Peripatetically, sir, perhaps. Mr. Rosher subscribes to

the view that Mrs. Grebshaw and the people at Pilbeam
House are perhaps suspect in some way. My own view
inclines more to the—er—view that she calls there, and
has for some time, as helper. Part of the religious sect. If
she *is* engaged in underhand matters, it will be merely
concealment of her husband's financial transactions. *If*
she knew anything about them. And I am not convinced
that she did. We know nothing against her."

"Is there," the Chief asked, "a back way into the
house?"

Neither could tell him for certain. Grinly spoke again.
"I expect so, there's always a back gate somewhere. And
they have this dancing team staying, she could have arrived with them in their coach."

"Mm." The Chief made display of considering for a few
moments. "Mm. Well—tempting though they may seem,
we cannot allow ourselves to explore sidetracks. We must
stick to our main issue, which is murder. I don't see the
widow, or a small-sized cleric, stabbing our man publicly
to death in a pub. Do you?"

They had to agree, they did not. So the matter was put
aside. A few minutes later the Chief offered more coffee.
It was turned down flat. The guests left, saying nothing to
each other as they came down the stairs and nothing
when they parted.

Curiosity in woman is endemic. It stirred in Mrs. Molly
Blenkiron when she came back from seeing a policeman
off to find her sister already grappling with the telephone. When Mrs. Grebshaw made it clear, and very
snappily, that the call had nothing to do with her she took
it, frustrated and touched with pique, into the living
room, where she remembered that she put a kettle on, to
make tea.

120

She went through into the kitchen. No harm done, the kettle was electric with a switch-off device operating when the water boiled. She reset it, fetched the tea-making materials, and stood by. Made herself a cup and sorted out a chocolate one from the biscuit tin, expecting that her sister would join her at any moment. When she did not, even after biscuit and tea were gone and she had poured a second cup, she said to herself. *She must surely be finished by now. You can't help wondering, can you, her rushing to the phone like that as soon as he was gone? Wonder who she was ringing. And not coming in for a cup. You can't tell me that's natural. And she looks dreadful. She's ill. I'm sure she's ill.*

Has she gone back to bed? Without telling me?

That's not like her, when she's ill everybody hears about it. She hasn't changed that much since we were kids, she's even rung me before now to moan because she had a cold.

You couldn't call him handsome, that Rosher, but he's a real man. A real man, all right. I do like a man who's a proper man.

I've had nothing, really, since Arnold died.

Didn't have much before that. Not for years.

Even in the early days he wasn't very good at it.

They do say that even when a man looks as though he would be, he isn't always.

I wouldn't know, I never had one.

She must *be finished by now. I'll take a cup up.*

Well, I can't just let her lie there.

She carried the tea up on a tray, small pot under a woolly cozy, cup and saucer and a plate of biscuits. Her sister was in the double bedroom wherein she would never sleep with Harry again, but not in bed. She stood at the wardrobe clad only in underwear. Dressing robe and nightgown lay crumpled on the floor and she was reaching in for a dress.

Mrs. Blenkiron said, "I've brought you a cup of tea. Thought you might have gone back to bed."

"Why should I go back to bed?" The snap in full evidence.

"Well—you look a bit seedy. That's all."

Mrs. Grebshaw said nothing. She fetched out a dress and held it up, to lower it over her head. It was then, as the hem of her slip lifted, that her sister noticed the little cluster of marks behind her knee and thought, with a twitch of alarm: Fleabites? Never! The house is clean enough, she was always one for that. Maybe she picked one up somewhere. In a bus.

She put the tea tray down on the dressing table, without mentioning the matter. Hostesses do not take kindly to hints that the house is crummy. The dress Mrs. Grebshaw had donned fastened at the front. The zip done up already, she was reaching for a hat from the shelf above the hanging space, lifting it, to place it on her head.

Mrs. Blenkiron said, "Are you going out?"

"Yes."

"I was going to get some breakfast. You ought to have some breakfast—"

"I don't want any breakfast." The hat was on, little hair-wisps were being stowed away.

"But—"

"I don't *want* breakfast!" Too much volume in it, too violent the delivery.

"Oh. Well—please yourself." And Mrs. Blenkiron left.

She did not exactly flounce out, but she was annoyed. All very well for her sister to tell her to shut up, this had been normal traffic all through their lives; but for Edna to blow her out so brusquely—yes, it was aggravating. She went back to the kitchen to smooth her feathers with

122

more tea. While she was there she heard the front door close and knew her sister had gone. Without farewell or even a mouthful of cornflakes.

Pity she did not then know the significance of those "fleabites" behind Mrs. Grebshaw's knee. Had she known, and phoned Rosher about it, a great deal of trouble might have been circumvented.

But not until evening did she adjust her thinking. Long before that she bought a discreet preparation, and wafted it about a bit. When she came upon a small, plump plastic envelope containing a white powder, tucked away on the hat shelf of the wardrobe, she believed it had something to do with headaches. It concerned her more, when she came wafting into the bedroom, to find that her sister had not so much as nibbled a biscuit or even drunk her tea. What has come into a woman, that she scoots without drinking her tea?

Before the banks were open; before the police could start their visiting in pursuit of Harry's hidden treasure; before the Chief Constable's meeting; well before Mr. Grinly, working alone, had tracked all those phone numbers from Harry's pad and decided that none of them connected to people known to the records; just before the end of the morning service conducted by the Reverend Edgar P. Mitten, Mrs. Grebshaw arrived at Pilbeam House. Entering posed no problem. Before the dancers left and after they came home, exterior doors were left unlocked, to facilitate their prancing in and out.

She entered the glittering shrine as they came toward the end of their closing hymn, copyright Reverend Makepiece Ewart (Founder, Friends of the Most Mighty Brother) all unauthorized reproduction (including public performance) forbidden. At meetings in all the Brotherhood's gatherings it was used as closing hymn, but not always so effectively as here, led by the resonant bass of the Reverend Edgar P. Mitten; which bass rose and fell in the manner of Jim Reeves before he went to explain it to his Maker, the lesser piping of the congregation wobbling less certainly after.

> *O Mighty Giver, couched above,*
> *Look down on us, we pray-hay-hay,*
> *And from Thy throne of perfect love*
> *Wash all our sins away-hay-hay.*
> *Teach us to dance and we will dance*
> *Throughout each perfect day-hay-hay,*
> *Bid us to go and we will go,*
> *To stay and we will stay-hay-hay.*

It goes to a stately measure. Every other line ends in three crotchets, the next starting on the last beat of the four-quarter bar. This accounts for the "hay-hay." The aspirate is not written in, but refuses to remain silent. Five verses in all. This is believed to better by one the Anglican Doxology.

The Reverend Mitten, facing the congregation from in front of the fairground-bright altar, saw her come in. The mellow bass never faltered; but his mind said: The stupid cow. The stupid, stupid cow.

He could see young Tony's eyes moving above his singing mouth, marking her out as she entered—all the eyes were, naturally—and coming back to linger upon him—questioningly? Reflectively? Young Tony and his little bird frightened him. He was not even certain who they were. Cold and competent killers, that was for sure. Sent by the big people—in the States? In London?—as swift reply to his call, arriving as part of the dancing team visiting from the city branch of the sect set up by Reverend Makepiece Ewart in person when he was over for the mission last year, dealing contemptuously with Harry Grebshaw almost as soon as their tent was up.

And that fucking dog. He didn't like that fucking dog. The silly cow looked very sick.

She remained standing just inside the door while the hymn drew to its close and he pronounced the final blessing. "May the All-Harmonious Giver fill our hearts and minds with harmony this day and always, and may we hold in our hearts the harmonious love of our Mighty Brother." They all cried amen and hallelujah and began to troop out, greeting her beamingly as they went by. "Good morning, Sister Edna," they said, and "Hello, Sister Edna." She made some sort of reply, twitching her white lips at them. Only young Tony and the girl Jennifer hung back, the lad pretending to retie a shoelace.

When the congregation was gone, the Reverend Mitten moved down to her, hissed in an undertone, very aware of the young couple advancing now between the seats, "What the hell are you doing, coming here now?"

She flinched at the attacking tone, his whole ensemble of voice, body, set face and hostile eye. "I—needed to see you," she said. "The—the police came—"

"I know, for Christ's sake! You told me on the phone."

He knew what she was here for, all right. She needed a fix, she came for the needle. And sex, no doubt—he shouldn't have shouted at her yesterday—he knew women; now she'd keep demanding it. They did, when some unguarded act made them fear you no longer loved them.

Well, she surely wouldn't get that. All the things he had on his mind, he wouldn't be able to perform.

He looked upon her with new loathing, the white,

black-eyed face, the twitching lips, and thought, I must have been mad to start it in the first place. I ought to know better by now than to mix women with business. If it hadn't been for women, I might have been anything by now.

When the affair had started, there had been genuine flame. Now—oh, so common a situation, especially under stress—the flame was out in him, but not in her. It was snuffed in him abruptly when her husband caught them at it. Who'd have thought that oaf loved her so much.

Well, he must have done, he went mad with jealousy. Mad—mad. They'd had it made here, all sewn up—and he was fixing to throw it all away. More than that—if London acted as normal, they could all have been killed. If he had not told what he was going to do, if she hadn't heard him doing it over the phone and passed word on— he *would* have. He'd have destroyed them all.

She said, "They've taken his checkbook away—they say he's been gambling."

"I know, I know, I know." He'd have handled the matter with far more of his practiced urbanity but for the unsettling loom of Tony, cold-eyed at his back. The young man said icily, "Get her upstairs."

"Yes. Yes." The Reverend Mitten took her arm, turning her toward the door. "Come on—come on—" Belatedly, he added, "—darling."

They left the garish shrine, all of them. Nobody snuffed a candle or knocked up a switch to save expense. The little man's eyes dodged about as he led her across the room and up the stairs, but nobody appeared. The dancers had scattered to rooms and tents and were gathering ribboned hats, cloglike footwear, corn pads, whatever they would need during the day. The young couple went by the side passage, through the back kitchen door and so to their tent, where the dog greeted them with the restrained boisterousness manifest when affection is reciprocal and governed by good training.

The lad donned his boots and sat caressing the black delighted ears while the girl fiddled with hair and dress, as women must before they go out.

He said, "I'll ring London as soon as we get into town. I don't like the way things are going. She looks as if she's cracking up, and he's got the shits."

"What if they say get rid of him?" She was adjusting her red sash.

He shrugged. "So?"

"There's a snag—they want the house. He's seeing to that. We *need* the house—the stuff'll be at sea by now, there's no time to divert it. Nowhere to divert it to."

"Why do we have to divert it? It can come in here, whether he's here or not."

"Yes, but how do we get it out again? We'll be bang at the center. And we're scheduled to leave Sunday, with these clowns. If he disappears now—you think they won't call the police? They'll be all over the place. A murder and a disappearance, both centered on here? And us still around?"

"Not just a pretty face," he said.

"You be glad you've got me to do your thinking. You can't just knock him off. *I* think he'd be all right if it wasn't for the woman. *She's* the danger—her we don't need."

"Knock her off?"

"We don't knock anybody off without London's say-so. I don't like the way we had to do the husband—if we'd had time to plan it properly, they'd only be looking for a missing person. They wouldn't even have bothered yet. I

127

never do like these emergency jobs, they never get done properly."

From outside the tent, a female voice called with appalling archness: "Are you two young people coming? The coach is here."

"On our way," the girl called back. She picked up her ribbon-decked straw hat. "When you speak to London," she said, "make sure you give them the full picture."

"Yup," he said. "Right. Look after the house, Herman. Git over, you daft old sod." He pushed the pleading dog aside and followed her out through the flap.

She spoke again, very softly, as they moved after the main body of dancers toward the path running round the house to where the coach would be. "Another thing—without him, who's going to keep the old lady under? Soon as she's recovered she's going to the fuzz. We want to be well clear of here."

"Maybe we should vanish him Saturday night. Just before we leave."

"See what London says." Oh! She stopped in her tracks on the path, pretty eyes widening, mouth a delicious O. "Hang on a minute—I forgot to say good-bye to Herman."

14

Half an hour farther into the day, Detective Inspector
Rosher set out to visit the bank where Harry openly oper-
ated that little account. He rang through to Detective Superintendent Grinly before he did so, to let him know
that he thought he would, and Superintendent Grinly
dealt quite stuffily with him. Said, well—it was up to him.
Not much point, if you've got nothing else to do, in getting corns on your arse, he said. Just so long as I know
where to get hold of you. He then clicked the switch. One
cannot expect to be beamed upon by a senior rank when
one just wrong-footed him with a Chief Constable.

The fact is, to be out on the street is to be away from
the desk; and Rosher, in common with all active detectives, hated desks, his own above all. Particularly in fine
weather. Somebody had to visit Harry's bank. Why dele-
gate, when the sun shines?

The visit yielded nothing, in the direct sense. He spoke
with the bank manager and such of his staff as had known
the late Harry as well as people on one side of the mon-

eybag normally know people who come regularly to the other, making small deposits and withdrawals. And that is all they knew of him. Yes, this is his only account. Yes—yes—it does appear that the last transaction took place about a year ago. Yes—here it is, confirmed on the printout. Dreadful thing, his getting stabbed like that. Really, one hardly likes to go out after dark. As for all these robbers in shotguns and balaclavas—well—he'd told his staff to take no chances. Furthermore, he twitched at Rosher as he said it. Notoriously nervous man, especially over lending money.

The stroll back to the station made it all worthwhile. It led him through the town center by way of a square set about with roses and those regimented flowers bred in square boxes by grim trade-union gardeners for the delight of perambulating town concils. They are used to set off concrete lamp standards that bend over at the top and turn everybody green and leprous by night. He mused as he came durable-suited and black-hatted—it was too balmy a morning to do more than muse—over the fact that Harry had left his honest account alone without ever bothering that it gathered no interest, from about when he started to gamble largish sums; and in the open center of the square he found a small crowd, watching bobbing ribbons. The ribbons and the hats they were attached to looked familiar. He moved on, to where he could see over the shoulders of short spectators.

Yes—they were familiar. This was the dancing team billeted at Pilbeam House, dancing hop-skip-and-bash-your-foot to a button accordion and a drummer with a bandage on his thumb. Having hopped, skipped, and bashed a foot, they hop-skipped again and bashed the other before clogging away in a ring, up and down and round about.

He stopped on the fringe of the crowd, running his eye

130

over the performers. Several were recognizable, in a vague sort of way, from when he saw them briefly as they came from the coach at Pilbeam House. One in particular gave him again that unfocusing memory-twitch: the lovely young girl smiling, achieving grace in spite of heavy footwear, intent upon her dancing. He frowned. A rattle came from beside him, and a bright female voice said, "Bless you, Brother."

It was a fat lady wreathed in smiles, buttoned into the team uniform. She carried a collecting tin and had shaken it to produce the rattle. He ignored it.

He said, "That girl. The pretty one—there. Who is she?"

"Where?" the lady said. "Oh yes—that's Jenny. Sister Jenny. *Isn't* she splendid? Natural dancer. You would never believe, would you, that she joined us less than a week ago, and she didn't know *one* of our routines. Very keen, of course—well, they both are—"

"Both?"

"Yes. That's her husband—the young man over there— Tony—" Rosher looked. The young man stood with his back toward him, chatting with a group of dancers not required for the current production. "He is extremely keen, too. Not up to our more complicated sets yet—but she is. Great gift from our Mighty Giver. They practice very hard, of course, in the evenings and so on. Remarkable progress. Bless them. And bless you."

She rattled the tin again. How was she to know that the man was more likely to ask for her collecting license than to put anything in? He still had his Earl Haig poppy from last year, ready for brushing up on November 11.

He said, "Where do they come from?"

"The city," she said. "We all do. We're from our city temple. We're staying here. Just for the week, you know."

131

There's this to be said about double-chinned Christian ladies, the ones who beam: They gush forth all you want to know and more, they live in full spate regardless of denomination. Many a male Christian married to one hears night and day the whispering Devil, saying: Bury a hatchet in her head. Rosher asked another question, still seeking to fix the girl in his mind.

"Joined you a week ago, you say?"

"Yes. Well—Friday. We came here on Saturday, of course. So it's not really a week yet, is it? Fancy—and just look at her, you'd think she'd been doing it all her life. Such a lovely young couple . . ."

The young man had turned into handsome profile, smiling at the girl. He gave her a wave. She smiled back, obviously having a wonderful time. Neither looked toward Rosher, who grunted "Thank you," and moved on. The collecting lady thought whatever Christian ladies think when they mean sod you, mate, and rattled her tin at the next in line. "Bless you," she beamed. "Bless you— bless you—"

Walking away, the inspector thought, I know bloody well I've seen that face before. Yes—she nearly ran into me, up at Pilbeam House. Yes—yes—but before that— somewhere . . .

Young. None of the others were young. Young man. The lad Dennison said a young man was driving. . . .

What was the number of that car again? C—40—5? 6? STJ. He'd check it with young Dennison, when he got back.

The dance ended. A scatter of applause from the spectators lifted and died on the bright morning air. The young man stepped away from the group and waited alone until the laughing girl joined him.

He said, "Found a call box just round the corner. London says handle it as we see fit." He added, pleased by her flushed and smiling pleasure, "This dancing caper suits you. You look terrific. Gives me the horn just looking at you."

She laughed happily, radiant and a little breathless from her exertions. "Keep your mind on your business. When you get older, you're going to be a dirty old man."

That collecting lady had unwittingly supplied the police with false information. Married they were not. But even today, camping among Christians, it is better to let them think you are, when you share one tent and a big black dog.

When Detective Inspector Rosher had hung the black hat upon the peg provided, he reported to Superintendent Grinly that nothing much had come from his visit to Harry's bank. He did it via the intercom, having no particular wish to mount the stairs for eyeball-to-eyeball. Not that he shrank from it, his eyeball was ever unflinching; but he never did see the point in galloping about when you have nothing of value to impart.

Mr. Grinly accepted his report with a grunt, and added, "Anything else?" The inspector said no. The superintendent said right, and rang off. So obviously he, too, had no development to pass on. All those men peddling all those prints around the banks and building societies this far had come up with nothing.

Mr. Rosher did not hang up. He retained grip upon the receiver, broke connection with a hairy finger and dialed again. Called the CID room and had Detective Constable Dennison brought to the phone. "Got your notebook?" he said.

"Yes."

"Give me the number of that car again."

Constable Dennison held the receiver between chin and shoulder while he produced his notebook. "C 405 STJ" he said. He was feeling cock-a-hoop this morning, having arrested last night, by a piece of commendable detective work, a little bugger who had eluded him for months. Self-approval bolsters a man, and he was not face to Old Blubbergut's face, eyeball to his implacable eyeball; wherefore he made bold to add, "About that old lady— Mrs. Filby-Stratton—she wasn't feeble—"

But Rosher had rung off. Oh well—san fairy ann, thought Constable Dennison, who had studied French at school; and he hung the phone up and took himself off to court, where he must present his little bugger to the magistrate.

Inspector Rosher had not yet done with the phone. He switched from the intercom to his outside line and put through a call to the motor-licensing authority at Swansea. It took them five minutes to trace the owner of the car. "Neal," he said. "Is that with an *e*? Anthony James Neal, Flat 14, Hermitage Towers, Chichester, Sussex. Thank you."

The little eyes were sharp now with interest. Why would a man from deeper Sussex drive all this way just to ponce around the streets in a ribboned hat? There must be closer poncing grounds.

A lad, furthermore, who brought his wife to join a city team, neither of them, according to the fat lady, fully proficient? One more call with a request that the recipient ring him back, and he went up to see Superintendent Grinly.

15

In his bedroom at Pilbeam House, the Reverend Edgar P. Mitten had administered a fix to Mrs. Grebshaw. He had restowed the syringe and the trappings and waited awhile for it to take effect, to change the shape of her face, to straighten the hunched and trembling body; to settle her. Devoutly, he wished now that he had never hooked her on it.

He had done it at the time of peak mutual lust, to break down the inhibition in her that held them back from utter abandon in their first rompings. Hot though she was for it, she had these fears: of her husband's knowing, of her almost unawakened body's now whimpering, wet greed.

Well, it had worked. Too bloody well. If they had not been so frantically immersed they would have guarded better against discovery. Normally they did. Hubby usually went out in the afternoons—betting, the fool? Throwing his share of the old lady's money away as soon as he got it? It seemed so, now—and they could get down

135

to it without constantly raising the head to listen, doors and windows locked.

It was Mrs. Filby-Stratton's door that let them down. They had been at it for months, and if in him the urge was ebbing a little, in her it seemed to flame stronger than ever. On that afternoon she was out of her clothes and sitting straddle-legged on the edge of his bed almost before he had his own door locked; cupping her breasts in her hands, pointing the swollen nipples at him, demanding that they be kissed. High as a kite she was, and lovely with that loveliness that came as surprise whenever she was released from the drabness of her clothing.

All the waning lust came back, and he was in there like a ferret. And the door to Mrs. Filby-Stratton's room forgotten completely. Or, perhaps, over the months he had grown careless. Hubby was out, as usual.

What brought him back they never found out. Chance? Suspicion? He didn't say. The communicating door between this and the old lady's bedroom they never bothered to lock, she was too drowsy with dope to know what was going on anyway. But the outer door—that one they locked.

Not this time, though. Or—perhaps the bastard had a key? Used it now, crept through—to open the inner door as they gasped toward orgasm and to start roaring. Never did dogs hit by a bucket of water spring apart so rapidly. Too late for stemming, his seed was still springing when his feet hit the floor, and he didn't even feel it. Stood there gasping, not with joy but with shock.

Now he looked at the woman with loathing, seeing her as source of all his fret and worry. As had Adam, cringing to God in the Garden. But he kept any hint of it out of the fine voice, speaking to her gently. Setting her off could be catastrophic.

"You shouldn't have come here, not all upset like that."

"I had to. I needed—you. I needed—" A fix. She needed a fix.

"You could have chased the dragon a little, steadied yourself down before you came." To chase the dragon is to smoke heroin, rather than inject it. He'd given her a little, so she could do it at home. "We don't want 'em all seeing you upset. You've got some, for when you need it—"

"My sister's staying," she said. "She'd smell it."

"Ah. You'd better get rid of her." You can't keep appearing with the jitters.

"How?" she said, cheekily. "Like you did Harry?"

"Like *we* did. Or like *he* did—I didn't know he'd go out and—"

"Of course you did," she said. "That's why you rang London, remember? Because *he* rang the police, and *I* rang you, so *you* rang London."

"I had to. Didn't I? You agreed. He'd have blown it all—he *said* he was going to blow it all." Didn't attack me physically, as I feared he meant to, standing in the doorway and roaring. Attacked verbally—said even then that he'd blow the whistle. I thought he wouldn't—he'd destroy his own end and himself—but he did, he meant to; he waited until she was home with him, and berated her—and rang the police.

She was bold now. She cut in on him. "Never mind Harry. Harry's dead." All the worries and fear besetting her when she arrived had vanished, you see. The terrible, yearned-for relief that kills, in the end. "Poor Harry. He didn't even know, did he?"

He didn't know the main business, true; but he knew about the old lady—he'd helped rig the plastic skull, the hands that floated through her room in the night, his and

137

Edna's were the voices that muttered and chortled from the little cassette recorder set behind the curtains. He took—and gambled away, the fool, apparently—his share of the money coaxed and wheedled out of Mrs. Filby-Stratton by his wife while she was fuddled with fear and pills, payment for holy relics, for spiritual help in exorcising demons. He knew she would be terrified all the way to death, once she had signed the house over to the Brotherhood, after sufficient time had elapsed to make it respectable and to clear her body of drug-sign, leaving her corpse clean and dead from natural causes.

Whether he knew of the main business, of London and why they wanted the house, the Reverend Mitten was uncertain. She said he didn't; but—"He knew enough," the little man said.

"Well—now we don't have to pay his share," she said. "Know what? You can marry me. Can't you?"

Desperately he kept from view the alarmed uprush of fear and loathing. "There's nothing really to stop us," he said. "Later. When we're all back on even keel. Darling." His mind was saying: She'll have to go. I don't know how—I don't know when—but she's got to go.

From the next room came the thin, quavering voice of Mrs. Filby-Stratton, stirring out of induced sleep, crying for attention, for human comforting, for Sister Edna. Mrs. Grebshaw nodded toward the communicating door. "What are we doing about her? Carrying on?"

"I don't know." It was all so complicated suddenly, where it had been straightforward. Caution said too much attention is focused on Harry—on this woman—on the house—go easy. Greed—and the bent are incurably greedy—said all the groundwork done—all that money—sale of the house—you never had a chance like it—

Because the price of the house would be his, split with

her. And Harry. Who would not be needing his share. London—the States—they were very generous in these matters, to those who engineered them. Their interest was not in the cash value of the house, small change to them. They would buy it once it was his, and pay the money to him. That was the arrangement. Their interest was in its location—quiet and private, respectably fronted, lying in a pocket between the mess of motorways and main transport routes linking the coast not far away with London—all the big cities. Innocent worshipers arriving daily—great cover for the agents who would come when the word was given, to spread the network from this new base. The city temple shut down—it never had been satisfactory, from the delivery and transportation point of view—and he in charge, on commission. Later, perhaps, when he had proved his worth, recall to America and—*anything* was possible.

The house alone must be worth a hundred thousand. Pounds sterling. And even that was small nuts, measured against potential.

Surely to Christ he hadn't blown it? Because—look what they had done to Harry! All in a matter of hours—latched a hit man on to the dance team—innocent idiots from the city temple, with no idea of their church's true function, invited to visit to build credibility—and Harry was dead. Before the day was out.

Frightening.

Why—oh—*why* had he ever been fool enough to lay her? And to hook her for the sake of it? His prick had always been his worst enemy at times when success in one of his undertakings swelled his ego along with it, exalted him to belief in his own omnipotence. Sex roared up in him then, he needed a woman. Women. In his clergyman persona he could hardly go out hunting. She was—available. Woven into the enterprise. And he—

Hell—he'd done it again. He should have known—he should have known. But the tyrant between the thighs never learns.

The quavering cry came again. He said, "You'd better see to her."

"Do I give her another pill?"

"For Christ's sake, no. You nearly killed her last time. Just—talk to her."

"Waste of time, that is. She doesn't know what you're talking about."

"It quietens her down."

"Kissy-kiss, then." He kissed her, forcing his lips not to clamp tight, revolted now by her wet opening, her fleshy tongue. When he decently could he broke away. She picked up the nunlike robe and headgear she wore in this house to mark her out as one of the life-committed. "I'm coming, Sister," she cried, happy in her high. "Don't piss yourself, I'm coming. Sister Edna's here, dear, don't get your drawers in a twist."

She'll have to go, he thought. Crude bitch—how could I have . . . She'll have to go.

Mr. Rosher's visit to Mr. Grinly had not lasted long. The superintendent was busy by the time he arrived, studying, ticking and initialing reports coming in now from the personnel engaged in tracking down Harry's cache. All negative. None of the city banks, none of the local banks, none of the building societies recognized him from his picture.

After Rosher had finished speaking, the super was not being obtuse when he said, "Allowing that this Anthony James Neal is staying at the house, it does not constitute

140

any kind of proof that he, or she, or anybody else up there knows anything about the case we're working on."

"He was driving this car. With her in it." The inspector's brows were low. He had that dogged set to the lips.

"No law against that."

"I'm not saying there is. I'm saying there's reasonable suss."

"What about?" Not obtuse; but without doubt Rosher had succeeded in rubbing yet another superior the wrong way. The man thus rubbed sets a bristling mind against the rubber who stumps in to flourish-the material he used to do the rubbing.

The inspector could not give a definite answer. He was not trying very hard. Constitutionally incapable of oiling the waters he himself troubled, faced with bristling he bristled. "The bloke comes from Chichester," he jerked. "It's a bloody long way to come, just to hop about in the street."

Grinly pointed out, not without inner satisfaction, an obvious truth. "He *lives* in Chichester. He didn't have to come here from there. Some of these people, they spend their holidays doing it. Festival weeks in different towns—combine it with touring."

"He only joined this lot just before they came—"

"So? There you are, then. Probably traveled on from some other festival, there are folk societies, they send 'em lists." The super knew this. He had a son with a hillbilly hat out there somewhere, with a plangent guitar.

"They don't all stay at Pilbeam House."

"Is he part of the sect?"

The inspector opened his mouth to answer just as the phone rang. It is not often you get an uninterrupted conversation in your modern office. Mr. Grinly picked it up. Grunted. Held it out without a word to Rosher. Mr.

Rosher said, "Rosher." Listened a moment. Grunted. Handed it back. Spoke.

"Well—I thought I ought to tell you. It's all down to you, you're in the chair." Even this had more aggression in it than mollification.

"Look," said Mr. Grinly. "I'm not saying there might not be something going on up there. We'll keep it in sight, maybe get a discreet obbo on. Later. For now, we concentrate on the job in hand. Right?"

So terminated the meeting. There was a grunt after, and a stomping out; but so far as meaningful dialogue and the frank exchange of views was concerned, this was it. Mr. Rosher left without revealing that the phone call came in answer to his call. To Scotland Yard, Records. No copper in the country had filed so much as a whisper of Anthony James Neal. No need, the inspector thought, to mention the fact. It would only weaken his case.

As lunchtime drew near, a man of forty or thereabout walked into the blind courtyard-alley where the team coach stood all day. He wore a seaman's hat—it is more often a limp brown trilby than the peaked one so dear to Hollywood—with a T-shirt stenciled IDAHO STATE UNIVERSITY, and he carried a cheap suitcase. The knowledgeable denizen of any port would have known him for a seaman, by the cut of his slacks and general jib; but inland, he was just a man about forty in a trilby hat. Incongruous once, such a hat with such a T-shirt; but in this day and age, anything goes.

He walked into the alley quite openly, and round to the back of the coach, where he seemed to have no trouble in opening the enormous luggage trunk. Inside were several rucksacks, one or two cases, left in by the dancers and containing, probably, spare socks and even shoes—things

142

they might need during the day but did not want to carry with them.

The man moved them all to the back, so that the floor of the trunk would hinge upward, revealing beneath a well used for stowage of tool kit, wheel jack, and so on. Into the ample space he put the case. He lowered the floor panel, rearranged the baggage, relocked the trunk, and walked away whistling; leaving a fortune in drugs behind. That case was packed, as if with packets of salt. Worth the ransom of a very fat king, cut and out on the streets.

The young couple saw him coming a few minutes later. The team was grouped in the square, chatting and showing forth the beaming mutual bonhomie proper to Christians on holiday. Most of the folk groups lunched with welcome pints in the local pubs, but this would not be fitting; so they stoked on sandwiches and soft drinks. The handsome lad, the pretty girl stood alone at a little distance. Nobody thought it strange. They were a young couple, very much in love. Some said, on honeymoon. Honeymooners tend to stand alone.

They were not expecting him. They knew he was coming, it had all been arranged; but not for today. They greeted him as if he were an old aquaintance, appeared by chance. They shook hands, beaming upon him, and the young man said, softly enough to keep it private, merrily enough to convince the sliding eyes, "You're not supposed to be here until Saturday."

"Early in," the man about forty said. "Diversion. We were supposed to call at Calais, but they got a dock strike. The Old Man came straight on, we're picking up a cargo here."

They did not need telling that the sea is very mighty, and the unions more so. Consign goods to them and you subject them to risk, of nonarrival due to shipwreck or the Bermuda Triangle; of late arrival owed to storm, tempest, or good old cussedness; even early arrival, in unusually fair weather or because of ports cut from the schedule due to industrial action or the captain's being too drunk to notice. Nor did they need to wonder why the consignment had to be off the ship as soon as she docked. A fortune in dope and Customs hovering—you do not sit on your bunk, running it through your fingers. Early arrival did not matter anyway, so long as they knew the stuff was there. The lad said, "No problem?"

"No problem."

It would be nice to report that the man spoke with a foreign accent, because drugs smugglers are not the kind of people one longs to claim for one's own, but in fact he spoke with the twang of Brummagem. Learned his seamanship, perhaps, on the canals that wind, like a necklace of sump-oil, all round that terrible city. Well might a man go to sea, born in Birmingham. They shook hands with him again, and he went his way. For a night on the town—for a romp in a brothel—back to his ship—that was entirely his business. But you know what sailors are. They have not settled for making ships in bottles at forty or thereabout.

The lad Tony said to the girl, "We can get away tonight, then."

"No, we can't," she said. "Don't be daft."

"What's daft about it?"

"For a start, all our appointments are for next week."

"We could ring round. Refix 'em."

"*They'll* have dates set, to pass it on when we've delivered. London has it all set up. We're not going to foul it up with London. They told us to cut it on Saturday night, with Mitten. Give him his share, take ours and get it away

144

Sunday morning. With this lot." She nodded toward the dancers, now munching happily; smiled at a lady who was smiling at her with the salacious goodwill ladies extend to honeymooners.

"It was only supposed to be in the coach for a few hours—"

"What's the difference? It's safe enough there. We'll have a word with Tommy, he'll see nobody gets near it." Tommy was the coach driver. They hadn't met him before—few of a big organization's people actually meet. The less they each know, the less they can tell if they get busted and are foolish enough to talk—but he was one of them. London said so, when they were attached at short notice, to deal with Harry and to conduct a survey into the situation at Pilbeam House. To ride herd on the consignment and to take away, what was not booked to the Reverend Mitten, for delivery to dealers all over the country.

Big operation. And they functioned well within it. This week, folk-prancing Christians. Next week, they might be disco dancers—a rich young couple staying at the best hotel—art students—anything, anywhere. Good little performers.

"Yeah," he said. "I suppose you're right." Better where it was than to lug it about unnecessarily. "I'd like to get away from this lot, though. They're beginning to get on my tits, and I've got a bloody great blister."

She laughed up at him. "I like it. Haven't enjoyed myself out of bed so much in years. I might take it up as a hobby."

"Sod that," he said. "My feet aren't taking to it."

"You don't have to dance," she said. "You can always learn the accordion. Or the drum. Another thing you're

145

forgetting—we still have to decide what we do about Mitten and his woman."

"I could deal with that before we leave. Tonight." He was teasing. They'd be staying on. He was grinning down at her, and teasing. To the envious ladies, they looked like something out of Mills and Boon.

"You won't," she retorted. "We're not having any more of *that* sort of thing. Whatever we do, we do it properly."

He put an arm round her waist and they moved back to the group. The munching ladies beaming them back chewed upon envy. Not for them to question, but why— oh why—couldn't something like him have been given to them, and they as winsome as she?

The next time Mr. Rosher saw the house, he was not there by design. It stood back from the road to the big city, and he drove past without stopping soon after lunch, on his way to the city jail in response to a sudden urge to bare his breast by one of his clients there on remand. It happens quite commonly, the impulse occurring most often in those to whom the summoned officer has whispered that they might do a deal.

He had spent a fairly satisfactory hour with this client and a shorthand writer, and a time of friendly chat with his old friend alone in the barred, bleak interview room while the statement was being typed. A little signing, a little returning of old friend to small cell, a little passing through clanging doors, and he was out and about again.

This time he pulled in when he came to the house, on the opposite side of the main road from the gates. From here he could see very little of the building itself, just the roof and chimneys beyond those glum evergreens bordering the curving drive. He sat and debated with himself.

Should he call in? Surprise the little man again, lean upon him somewhat, see what he could rattle out?

Better not. Not now. For one thing: Information received from the old friend in the nick made it necessary that he return to the station for a word with one Bernard Fowler, even now being collected by squad car as result of his call from the city.

For another: Without backup, a man must be careful not to lean prematurely. Often, the unexpected lean is very effective. The leaned-upon tend to scatter, attempt to scarper, do silly things. Fine—so long as you are hidden away and watching, men tucked into odd corners all around to move in and mop up when you whistle. Without these men—very dodgy. Things can be burned—moved; alarmed people are given time, possibly a lot of it. And time is what they make good use of.

And a third thing: Leaning necessarily demands a certain earnest determination in the questioning. Should you be wrong, and the leaned-upon blameless, they tend to squeak; and Mr. Rosher did not wish it to be advertised by squeaking clergymen that he was bearing the black hat yet again along a private furrow, in the very face of Grinly, the Old Man, and all, when he had been told to keep his mind on a murder case.

No, he thought. No. Better leave it. And he drove on.

A pity he could not get right into that house, no holds barred. He would have found, in the cellar, scales for weighing and all the substances needed to cut high-grade heroin, including little plastic bags. A small quantity of the drug itself in the Reverend Edgar P. Mitten's adopted bedroom, together with the syringe that had made a flea-pattern behind Mrs. Grebshaw's knee. He would have found the system of wires by which luminous hands and a grinning skull floated across Mrs. Filby-Stratton's room by night, and the cassette recorder loaded with the tape that muttered and cursed, cackled, chortled, moaned, threatened. He would have found the skull and the hands, plastic from a joke shop, made in Hong Kong.

Among the animal matter he would have found, in one bedroom, Mrs. Grebshaw, blood full of drug, asleep now and snoring lightly on the Reverend Mitten's bed, and he standing by wondering should he give her another shot—an overdose—smuggle the body away somehow; in the adjoining room a ravaged old lady, also asleep and under influence, hopelessly hooked by now; and, if he explored at the back, a big black dog in a tent, faithfully mourning through the day.

Pity. Pity he couldn't go in. Such a bag of goodies comes the policeman's way but rarely. If he could not get actually in, it's a pity he was not sitting there in his car an hour or two later, when a girl came out, walking that big black dog. He might, as things tumbled together, have realized where he saw that face before, the memory was obscured only by her modern gender-bending.

Now *that* would have been worth a warrant.

16

They returned from the town at the usual time, and the dog bayed deep joy long before they entered the tent. But he did not rush out to greet them. Disciplined by his own loving anxiety not to incur displeasure, the basic of all good training, he waited, booming adoration. Even when they came in he did not jump up and slobber; but it was a damn close-run thing, the desire to do so, twisting his body into groveling ingratiation-shapes, his voice a frantic whimper. All day alone in a tent, worrying—it's hard on a dog; but he stayed. Because he'd been told to stay.

The girl made more fuss of him than the young man did. This was not because the lad thought less of him—he patted him, spoke to him affectionately, caressed his ears; but it is in the nature of women to drop to the knees, offer the face to the frantic tongue, croon and cuddle; and the wise man lets her get on with it. Tony crossed to his sleeping bag, sat down, and took off his shoes and socks.

He said, "If we're going to this caper tonight, I've got to

have a bath. Trouble with this joint, you can never get near the bloody bathrooms." Two of them. Always occupied.

"You've only just had a shower." By arrangement, several of the teams used the municipal showers, their alloted times governing time of return from town. No good dancing again once the sweat is washed away, and those who came late had had it until the following day.

"It's the feet," he said. "The bloody feet." He was massaging them, waggling the toes.

"You haven't finished with them yet, Herman's got to have his walk. Who's a good boy then? Good boy—good boy—" This to the groveling dog.

"You take him, huh? I need to soak 'em. *If* I can get near the bathroom."

"You don't have to. Do it in the bowl. Plenty of hot water in the kitchen. Fetch a bucket over."

"I'll be glad to get back to civilization. Bloody stripwashes and bloody buckets—"

"It's got its points, though," she said. "I like washing you all over. I like you doing it to me."

"Wait till I get you back in the bath at home," he said. "Puts me off, I keep finding ants and bits of grass under the foreskin."

"I hadn't noticed, you've been working well. Maybe it tickles you up." The dog went sobbingly, ecstatically mad as she reached for his lead. "Hold still, Herman. Hold *still*, good, good boy, while I clip you on. That's a good boy. Goo-ood—good boy. Here we go then. See you later."

This is when Rosher should have been about: to see her cross the road with that big black dog walking wonderfully to heel; along a little and through a gate into a field, where she let him off the lead to gallop and grin and

150

gambol, and lie with lolling-tongued laughter all over him when she told him to stay, and walked away, and called from a distance; and praised him to his overjoy as a good, good boy. No livestock about, no sheep. He would not have worried them anyway, however his red mouth watered. A word from her, he'd have lain down and stayed until he died.

When she took him back to the tent she said as she came in, "He's got the woman in the house. I saw her at his bedroom window."

"The bloody fool must be crumpet-struck. What's he got her up there for this time of day? They'll have been having it away before we got back." He was lying barefoot on his sleeping bag, a bowl of water standing by unemptied. The dog sniffed, and began to lap at it.

The girl pushed his nose away. "No, Herman—no. Dirty. I don't see what he sees in her."

"One man's meat is another man's poison."

"Meat? Thank you very much."

"Not you. You're more like chicken, all tender and succulent." He made a leer. She liked it. "*I* can't see what she sees in him."

"The voice. Makes it twitch."

"Not mine, it doesn't."

"And the novelty. We like to find out if it's true about little men."

"One thing's true about him. He's a pain in the arse. I still can't decide what to do about him."

"You can't do anything before Sunday. We'll have to come back, we can't disappear him with all this lot around."

"From Sunday on we'll be busy. We won't be able to get back for a week. If she's cracking up and hanging around here all the time—you know what they're like when they get to that stage—*she* could have blown it by then."

"Perhaps we ought to concentrate on her. She could go. Rig it right, that might not have to wait till Sunday. And it might bring him back into line. Long enough for us to fix with London to send a replacement over. Then we could deal with him safely, he could just have been recalled to the States. Another Yank clergyman taking over, it'd look right."

"Yeah, I'd thought of that. It'd mean another body, though, wouldn't it? And the other one's her husband."

"There wouldn't have to be a body. Vanish her."

"Yup. That might be the way to work it. Only, we don't have a lot of time to plan it. Ask me, London slipped up putting 'em in here with him."

"London can't guarantee every tiny Tom, Dick, and—Harry—oh—ha-ha—can they? They were already working —they wouldn't have been more than twopenny half-penny peddlers—and London was looking for a safe house. They'd have put the word out—and these Greb-whatever-their-name-is must have known the situation here and put the plan up. So London got on to the States—the States organized the mission or whatever it was—little man came over with it—I suppose they rented the house and took it from there. Wouldn't mind betting the city tabernacle or whatever they call it is only a tempo-rary base, they'll just have been using it until they were dug in here. Bet it'll vanish within a month."

Shrewd girl. Good thinking. This was almost the full picture of what happened and was scheduled to happen. She was aided, of course, by their having worked for the organization for some time; but even so, she had applied her brain and privately sorted it out, entirely from obser-vation of their methods. Other desirable properties had been acquired, all taken over from elderly or feeble owners. It had not taken her long to tumble what was going on here. And he was no idiot.

He said now, surprising her, "They're a couple of creepy bastards, it won't be any grief to deal with 'em. Gets up the hooter a bit, what they're doing to the old lady."

"Well, well," she said. "Aren't you the one who knifed the husband?"

"That's different. He was a man. And he didn't suffer, I never make 'em suffer. This is dirty."

Up rose an overenthusiastic voice from outside. You could hear the love-happy beam that went with it. "Coach leaves in ten minutes, everybody. Coach leaves in ten minutes."

"Better get your gear on," she said. "Oh—look, Tony—look how he all droops, he knows we're going out. We'll be back, darling. We'll be back soon. Good boy. Good, good boy." She laid a peach-bloom cheek against the dog's face, put lissome arms around him, hugged him, crooned to him. The dog sighed deeply, and ate his heart out.

"Why don't we take him with us?" he said.

"Do you think they'd mind?"

"Why should they? They're supposed to love every bloody thing, aren't they? Sod 'em, if they do."

The pity is that Molly Blenkiron did not contact the police sooner to report a small packet of white powder found tucked away in her sister's wardrobe. A call in the morning, and they could have sent a couple of drugs-squad men down to take it into custody while other men proceeded to Pilbeam House armed with a warrant, all in seemly fashion according to the book. It would have saved so much uncouth kerfuffle. Alas, having decided

the stuff had to do with some facet of female frailty, probably headaches, she put the packet back and forgot all
about it. Until the evening.

She thought of Rosher, though, and of her sister; of
how sick she had looked, of her sudden departure without even a cup of tea taken; of the surprising and rather
nasty fact that she appeared to be harboring fleas. That
sort of thing wasn't like Edna at all, she'd always been
clean enough. She must have picked one up somewhere.
On the buses, which traveled through ethnic minority
areas.

She went out to the shops, where she bought that discreet powder. She puffed it about, wardrobe, bed, under
cushions; in her own bed, certainly in her own bed. When
there was none left, she stuffed the container well down
in the rubbish bin.

She made the beds, she Hoovered a little, she hummed
a little. She wondered what to have for lunch. She wondered if her sister would be coming home for a bite.
Thinking of a bite brought her back to fleas.

Perhaps it wasn't fleas, perhaps it was—unthinkable!
Unthinkable!—bedbugs. She wondered if the powder was
effective against bedbugs, and dug the container out
again to read the label.

Effective against *all* problem parasites, it said. She
hoped she'd bought the right stuff, you cannot ask the
girl in the shop. You ask for what you trust it is and hurry
away in a hot flush, not lingering to read the label and to
ask whether the term "problem parasites" includes the
flea and the common bedbug. You can't even say you are
inquiring for a friend.

Edna did not return for lunch. Mrs. Blenkiron had thin
toast, with a smidgeon of marmite. And coffee. Black. No
sugar. She stayed plump in spite of it. Afterwards she sat

154

down with her feet up, the radio on, and Inspector Rosher floating about in her mind. After lunch was her sexy time, and she did like a man who *was* a man.

Fret about her sister set in around teatime. She should have been home by now. Or she should have rung, or something. Betting was, if she hadn't been run over, she was at Pilbeam House. The police had the telephone number pad still, but a small stack of tracts stood on the hall table. "To LEARN how YOU!!! may yet be SAVED!!!!" it said in black, "RING THIS NUMBER!!!!" And it gave the number in red. She rang it.

Had the Reverend Edgar P. Mitten been able to prevent it, Mrs. Grebshaw would never have answered the phone; but she happened to be passing on her way to the lavatory when it rang, so she paused and picked it up. "Hello," she said quite gaily.

"Is that you, Edna?" asked Mrs. Blenkiron.

"Sister Edna speaking."

"Are . . . Good. Are you all right, dear?"

"All right? Why shouldn't I be all right?"

"No. Well—you looked so ill this morning—"

"I *was* ill this morning. Now I'm beautiful. It's all beautiful."

"Ah. Good. When are you—I thought you might be home by now—"

"Home? Where's home? In my Father's house are many mansions. Well—I can't stand here all day chattering, unless you want me to piss myself." A giggle, truncated as the line went dead.

Mrs. Blenkiron gazed at the receiver in shock. Ladies who are not pop-groupies do not publicly, in coarse Anglo-Saxon, refer to the danger of imminent involuntary bladder operation. Christian ladies decidedly refrain. Mrs. Grebshaw never, *never* had used such a phrase, not within

155

her sister's memory. Even her lavatory seat wore a discreet yellow garment, the toilet-roll holder a bonnet to match. Daily she slaughtered 99 percent of all known germs with a plastic can, and the whole place smelled of pear drops.

It was—weird. The whole conversation was—weird, from the Sister Edna opening to the closing giggle; and still, in Molly Blenkiron, the mental penny did not drop.

Drop came in the evening. Seriously concerned now by her sister's not returning, she turned on the television, more for distraction than for entertainment. A cops-and-robbers series passed before her eyes, hardly registering until it sat her up straight with a sequence showing the cops in the bedroom of a dead young junkie. The camera traveled slowly up the half-naked body, lingering on the legs; and behind the girl's knee was a grouping of what looked like fleabites. Bug bites. Problem-insect bites. The script identified them as the marks left by mainlining. Riveted, she saw the scene change to a warehouse where a trio of schoolgirls heated, on a piece of cooking foil, white powder shaken from a plastic envelope similar to the one upstairs, taking it in turn to inhale the smoke through a thin tube.

Oh my God! she thought, and went upstairs. There was the plump envelope; and deeper delving among the things neatly folded and stacked on the wardrobe shelf uncovered a plastic tube and one of those foil cups used by Mr. Kipling to contain exceedingly good cakes, with some kind of residue in the bottom.

She had pretty hair. At the nape of her neck it was rearing up. She had no experience of drugs, all she knew was that they kill. The newspapers, the television—that show still flickering on toward shootout where all the bullets go *wha-a-ang–wheeeee*, the radio—all screamed about

156

it. Everywhere, at all hours of the day and night, ravaged people were dropping dead from them and lying about underfoot, or expiring on a squalid brass bed in a filthy hovel. Everybody knew that. Bishops deplored it on "Thought for the Day," for five minutes in the early morning.

Her mind went jumping about. She knew this much: that the penalty for having drugs in your house is draconian. She said in a panic: It wouldn't be Edna—it must have been Harry. Harry brought it in. I never did trust Harry. But she knew that she lied—her sister's sickness— the coarse gaiety on the phone . . .

Pilbeam House! That's where she got it—she'd had some between leaving here and answering the phone. And Harry—both of them—worked there. . . . This lot she was mixed up with—Arnold always said, never trust a Bible-basher.

She thought: *I must get rid of this. Edna will be—angry— that I've been in among her things—but—I can't let her—she looked terrible. I'll have to—tell her I know—ring her—get rid of this first. . . .* Hurriedly, she carried the powder, the tube, the foil cup to the lavatory and flushed them away. Had to wait for the cistern to refill and poke the cup down with the toilet brush to make it vanish, because the first time it bobbed up, floating.

Now she tried again to ring her sister. No answer. She'd try again later. She went back into the living room.

The television show was just reaching its end. Dope men bursting in to murder one who grassed; shrieking up of police cars; shootout, with all the bullets going *wha-a-a-ang— wheeeee.* Arrests, bodies, and a homily from the chief cop, a crusty man with the heart of a hush puppy. Evil trade, he told his admiring juniors, who appeared to love him very much in spite of his manners. Evil men—stop at nothing—murder and mayhem—Fade-out, credits, and a commercial for Birdymix, which keeps your budgie bouncing.

Somebody there to talk with, she might have acted differently; but she was all on her own in a state of high agitation; and fear came down on her. Murder and mayhem. If she rang, and told Edna she knew, THEY might turn up here—Edna might tell them—they'd come to silence *her*—they might kill Edna, too—her and Edna both.

Irresolute, she hovered over the phone; and then she called Rosher. Through a handkerchief.

She was lucky to find him there; although, had he not been, perhaps any copper would have done. She asked for Inspector Rosher because he was the one she knew, and very much on her mind, and a woman in distress turns still toward the strong man she fancies and fantasizes; but she gave no name.

He was working late only because the little man he had hurried back to interview had proved more stubborn than expected. He broke, though, and Mr. Rosher was in his office dealing with the necessary paperwork, well into overtime, when the phone rang. He said, "Put it through," and identified himself when the switchboard WPC said go ahead. The phone spoke very briefly.

"Drugs! Drugs! They've got drugs at Pilbeam House!"

He knew the voice. You *can* disguise a voice on the telephone with a handkerchief, any cops-and-robbers viewer knows it; but not by simply stretching the thing over, which is what she did, knowing no better. All you do that way is reduce the volume a little. The little-girl tone was there, the panic was plain. He said: "Mrs.—er—"

But she was gone. She'd hung up and was standing by the phone, shaking all over, realizing that what she had succeeded in doing by this panic measure, designed to save her sister and herself from whatever, was to grass that sister into nick along with the rest if the police went to Pilbeam House and found her drugged, all among the drugs.

She must ring—she must warn Edna to come home at once, to be not there for longer than it took to clamp the hat on.

She dialed with a fumbling finger. No reply again.

Mr. Rosher had no trouble with delayed penny-dropping. The coin fell with a clang, before the phone left the hairy ear. Thought is so very much quicker than action that ere the instrument was squarely in its cradle, he had thought as follows:

Drugs. That's it. There's the connection—that's where Harry was getting his gambling money—from just about when Mutton moved in. . . . The wife's told the sister—the sister's grassed. And Harry—would have been knocked off for—something to do with drugs—by—Mutton? No. Too conspicuous. A hit man, arranged by the big bastards? A young man from Chichester?

Not bad. Wrong on one point only: Harry's money came not from drugs, it came out of Mrs. Filby-Stratton. Also, of course, Mrs. Grebshaw did not tell her sister. Allowing for these minor blemishes, it was still a fair effort. A seasoned policeman starts from advantage, mind you. He knows about drugs, he knows the viciousness of the big men behind the trafficking, he knows human depravity. Who better? It's his stock-in-trade.

Mr. Rosher hardly let the phone settle before he lifted it up again. He rang Mrs. Blenkiron. Line engaged. She was trying to contact her sister at Pilbeam House. He gave it a few glowering moments, tried again. This time the sudden shrilling almost lifted her into the air as she crossed the hall away from it. She came back, dithered, picked it up. "Hello?" she said, heart going like a trip-hammer.

He barked straight into her ear. "You rang me."

"No," she said. No identity problem here. Just babbling shock. "No—no—no—I didn't—"

He did not bother to argue. She was clean. He'd have her brought in, she would soon spill in an interview room. His interest was not in her. "Is your sister there?"

"No. No—she's not—she's—out—"

"Where?"

A woman with a penchant for rough, tough men crumbles like apple charlotte when they bark. Especially when she is distraught and floundering, way out of her depth. And Rosher's was the ultimate bark. "I don't know," she cried. Tears were bursting out of her now, choking into her little-girl voice. "Pilbeam House—Pilbeam House—"

"Stay where you are," the bark commanded. "I'm sending some men round."

She didn't even leave the phone, poor thing. If he'd told her to jump up and down over her outstretched leg, she would have done it, until she was commanded to desist.

Mr. Rosher, having slammed his phone down, clicked the switch of his intercom, trying Superintendent Grinly's office. No reply. He clicked again, connecting himself to the duty sergeant who must record the comings and goings of CID personnel engaged in major cases. "Mr. Grinly. Gone home?"

"Been gone half an hour," the sergeant said.

Another phone call. Grinly's house, well out in the suburbs. "He's not here," Mrs. Grinly said. "He rang five minutes ago, a car ran into him. Came out of a side turning and ran into him. He's not hurt, but he said he'll have

160

to stay with it, it's bashed his wheels in." The car wheels, she'd have meant.

Well, he would. Statements to be made, measurements taken. Very thoroughly, in this case. Unlucky for some, that they drive out of a minor road smack into a police superintendent proceeding in orderly fashion along a major one.

"Thank you," said Rosher. "Will you ask him to ring the station when he gets in?" He switched back to intercom. "Call the car working Pumfrey Avenue. Number 4. A Mrs. Blenkiron, I want her brought in. And a Mrs. Grebshaw. If she's not there, leave a man. I want her as soon as she arrives." This in case she had left Pilbeam House by the time he got there. "I want another car outside Pilbeam House, just along from the big garage. On the road. If a woman comes out, I want her held there. When Mr. Grinly rings, I've gone up there."

The controller of these matters, scribbling busily, did not have to ask who was giving the orders.

Simple answer to the question, Why did Mrs. Blenkiron get no answer when she tried to ring the house?

Nobody heard the phone. It stood in the hall downstairs, and in these old, solid houses sound does not easily carry up stairs and through thick oak doors. Not when these doors are closed.

This is where the only people left in the house were, after the coach departed: upstairs in the Reverend Mitten's bedroom, he and Mrs. Grebshaw, with Mrs Filby-Stratton in the room next door.

In a sense, the clown who ran into Superintendent Grinly's motor messed up the book for Rosher; but there were many things he should have done, by rights, before leaving the station. He should, when he knew about Grinly, have notified the Chief Constable of the position; but he did not. The Old Man was at a reception in the big city. Rosher knew it; and he knew how one can swear that one telephoned the venue but was told the body required was not currently traceable, and that the message left was, quite obviously, not passed on. He should have called in the Drugs Squad. He did neither of these things. He left undone those things that he ought to have done.

The scent of kudos was in his flaring nostrils. Nobody could jump hard upon his foot for making a justified call at Pilbeam House seeking a lady said to be involved with drugs. If he questioned her there instead of having her brought in—he had the right—if the questioning spread to where it uncovered fish within the house—kudos must accrue.

To him. Not to a load of young scruff labeled Drugs Squad, who if they moved at all on his unsupported suspicion would probably screech up and cock everything. Not to Grinly, whom the gods had nobbled with a busted motor car. He could have this all to himself. That'd show bloody Grinly.

One thing you could guarantee with Detective Inspector Rosher: He could justify himself into anything, once he had been pooh-poohed and taken umbrage.

He could not, however, go it entirely alone. Not this time. Backing was needed, as indispensible witness. The squad car should be in position by the time he arrived; but if they had Mrs. Grebshaw, better that he send her back in it than divide the crew, taking one of them in with him. You never know what an arrested woman will do. If she takes to screaming and clawing, she can send a lone driver right off the road, and still claim molestation.

So he poked the black hat into the CID room on his way out. Three officers were there, pecking at typewriters. Two were female. That let them out. If God had meant women to be policemen, he'd have given them testicles. The other was young Wot'sname, who had come with him before. He'd do.

Rosher said, "You free?"

"Well . . ." Constable Dennison indicated the typewriter. He had just been in with another small rogue, and it all breeds paperwork.

"Get your hat."

"I was just doing a report—"

"It can wait."

Five minutes later they were driving through the town in Rosher's own car, the young man still not knowing where they were going, until the route taken said it had to be Pilbeam House. Here came the garage—there were the gates—and tucked away at obbo distance on the opposite side of the road, a squad car.

Rosher pulled in behind it. Got out and bandied forward, the constable at his heels. Said through the open window, "Haven't got her?"

"Nope," said the blue-capped man on the other side of the window.

"Anybody come out?"

"Nope."

"Hang on here. If I want you I'll call." The black hat turned to the acolyte. "Got your walkie?"

"Yes."

"Come with me." Line of communication established, away went the inspector, leaving his car where it stood. The shock value of a thunderous knock on the door works out at nil if a car has been heard to drive up. He

163

paused where the evergreens ended to take a long look at the house.

No sign of life. Constable Dennison mumured low at his elbow. "This used to be my old beat. Gone downhill since, she used to have a couple of gardeners. Lively old bird, she was. Had a live-in maid, too. And a handyman. Sort of chauffeur."

The inspector grunted. It didn't surprise him. If you are organizing a house for nefarious practices, first thing to do is get rid of the honest staff. Stands to reason. He stepped out from the concealing bushes and led on.

Upstairs, giving the kiss of life to Mrs. Filby-Stratton while Mrs. Grebshaw slumbered snoring on his bed next door, the Reverend Mitten shot upright when the thunderous knock came, with a gasp of pure terror. He thought at once of the police, but he dared not leave the old lady. There was life in her yet, the pulse was there. Faint—very faint—but fluttering there.

He had been with Mrs. Grebshaw in his bedroom, trying to persuade her not to strip off and climb into his bed, fending off her giggling advances, when he heard the old lady's sigh and dry gurgle from next door. He'd hurried in, while Mrs. Grebshaw carried on with her stripping; and he had been busy ever since.

She mustn't die now! Not stuffed with barbiturates. Not with the house full of people. Not for a month or two yet—not until she had signed the will and time had cleared her blood and old bones. He'd been careful not to inject her with anything—there were no marks on her skin; London would send a man when he requested it, to put a bubble in her blood or something—he didn't know how they fixed it. He didn't want to know, so long as she was dead from natural causes.

It was that extra pill—it was that crazy cow next door—

Hairy-knuckle thunder came again. The Reverend Mitten prayed most sincerely. O God, I can't go down, she'll be dead by the time I get back. Let them believe there is nobody in. Send them away, O God. Send them away. He lowered his sobbing mouth to the old lady's mouth again. He was no medical man, he didn't know what else to do.

The first part of his prayer was acceptable. The policemen did believe nobody was in. The second part was ignored. They did not go away. Inspector Rosher grunted, "Right, lad. Let's have a look at the back." He stumped away to where the path led off from the drive, round the side of the house. A door left open, maybe—a window—and bugger the warrant, let's poke about a bit inside while we've got the chance.

Before they reached doors and windows they saw motor cars. Several of them neatly parked beside a line of tents. Mr. Rosher checked the registration numbers, nodded to a rakish blue sports-saloon. "That the one you saw the woman in?"

He knew the answer. The number fitted. "That's the one," said Constable Dennison.

Of course it was. All the way from Chichester. The inspector grunted again, moving on to the back door.

If somebody had thought to bolt it, short of breaking a window they could not have got in. But what happy dancer bothers to bolt a back door, when a clergyman will be in the house all the time they are away? Somebody had turned the key, but a simple mortise lock is no match for an officer carrying a plastic credit card and his bunch of private keys. Every detective has one, illegal but winked at. Even Constable Dennison turned not a hair. His own bunch nestled in his pocket.

They came directly into the big, well-scrubbed kitchen. You could have eaten your dinner off the floor, had you been stupid enough. There'd be nothing of great interest here. They *might* store drugs in the flour bin, but in a house of this size, with storage cellars and many a nook and cranny, it was unlikely, especially with all the dancers about. Mr. Rosher led on again. Quietly, because one person at least was probably in the house. The old lady. When he saw her, she did not look fit to be taken out.

It did not bother him now whether anybody else was here or not. They were fish-smeared, they had not answered his knock. Challenged, complained against for unlawful entry, he would say that receiving no answer and knowing the old bird's condition, he came in to see that she hadn't collapsed, left all on her own.

He'd better just check the old girl. Mutton had taken her back upstairs when he was here before, that's where her bedroom would be. He made for the fine, curving staircase, Constable Dennison mounting behind him.

The first door tried was locked. Behind it, the Reverend Mitten did not even hear the handle turn. The next door opened. Inside lay Mrs. Grebshaw, stark-naked on the bed, out to the world and snoring dreamily. From the connecting door between this and the next room came faint sobbing, a sound as of breath being deeply indrawn; and silence.

Quite a pretty sight, Mrs. Grebshaw. Constable Dennison's eyes slid sideways as he followed his inspector, on to the open door.

Old Mrs. Filby-Stratton lay in a pink nightgown. Her bedclothes had been thrown back, and bending over with his lips glued to hers was the little clergyman. Both policemen thought for a mad, fleeting instant that she was being subjected to some perverted attack, but Mr. Mitten looked up panic-eyed, burbling, "She's dying—she's dying—she won't come out of it."

Rosher's bandy legs took him over the carpet fast. He barked, "Carry on!" Because mouth-to-mouth resuscitation can do no harm so long as you do not contract AIDS, even though it may do no good. He felt for a pulse as the clergyman's head went down again. It was there. The old girl was having a go. He turned his bark to Constable Dennison. "Ambulance."

"Yes," the constable said; and to Mitten: "Where's the phone?"

The little man squirted from the side of his busy mouth, "In the hall." But Rosher's thinking had leaped on. There is often delay when you ring for an ambulance. The crew is on tea-break, or all units are out, or they lose their way, when new one-way and no-go systems apply during Festival Week. Policemen know this better than most people.

He barked again: "Use your walkie. Get the squad car up to the front door."

The car would arrive for certain in a matter of seconds. Very much quicker, a one-way dash, than for an ambulance to cover the route out and back again. Even if it brought oxygen and all the gear for on-the-spot treatment, it takes time to manhandle and fit it. Get her to the hospital, where all they had to do was plug her in and switch her on.

Two minutes later, cocooned in blankets, Mrs. Filby-Stratton rested supine in Constable Dennison's arms as he bore her down to the car. "Keep the mouth-to-mouth going," Mr. Rosher commanded. "And come straight back here."

The young man's lips wrinkled involuntarily with repugnance at the thought of intimate osculation with that saggy, gummy old mouth. Her teeth were upstairs. He

167

was a game lad, though. "Yeah—right," he said. Verily, verily the policeman's lot is not a happy one.

"All right, sonny," said Mr. Rosher to the Reverend Edgar P. Mitten. "Let's have a look at your other one, shall we?"

"She's not mine," the clergyman burbled. "No—no—she's not mine—" Poor little bugger. Utterly gone to pieces.

He was, of course, in dead lumber. It had not needed deep thought to tell the inspector what kind of substances would keep a lady lying naked on top of a bed while a clergyman blew into an old lady in the next room. Lying in slumber so profound she did not even notice two great policemen tramping by, or the carrying out of that old lady.

Mr. Rosher now conducted the Reverend Mitten back upstairs and into his bedroom, where he pulled up one of the lady's eyelids and looked upon the pinpoint pupil with great satisfaction; while out on the main road, Detective Superintendent Grinly tucked away the documents handed back to him by a deferential patrol-car man and accepted the offer of a lift to his home.

Every policeman knows how to capitalize on psychological advantage. The little bastard was clearly shocked by what had happened to the old lady; and now that he had thought to spare for it, by the appearance of police. Double the punch, then. Start him babbling.

"Whatever you've been giving 'em," Rosher said, "you've overdone it. This one's in a coma. I wouldn't be surprised if they both die."

"It wasn't me!" cried the Reverend Mitten. "I swear—on my life—it wasn't me!"

The inspector was beginning to assume the air of avuncular jocularity used commonly by detectives toward the definitely bent, their own or those about to become their own. Out came the joke, but the simian face stayed grim, the little eyes hard. "Before I'm through with you, my son, you'll be able to swear on your life sentence."

Not a good joke. Ponderous. As a stand-up comic, the man would never have made a living. He had turned and was checking Mrs. Grebshaw's pulse. "Where's that phone then?" he barked. "You'd better hope she doesn't die before we get the ambulance here."

17

There is, operating in a field outside the town, a small aero and gliding club run by an ex-international speedway rider. He is a merry wight. In need of a good orthodontist, but he owns a shrewd brain. Every year, toward the end of the Festival Week, he stages a barbecue. One pound fifty a go. Most of the dancing and folk-singing people attend, by now it is almost traditional. His two or three instructors stand by, and those who fancy a flip pay on the spot and Bob is your uncle. Quite profitable. He is not supposed to serve drinks on the club bar to any but bona fide members, but the police like him, so once a year they turn a blind eye. He never gives any trouble.

On this fine warm evening they all enjoyed themselves. The young couple certainly did. They stayed on the ground because to fly would have meant leaving the dog whining and all upset; but they washed down their singed steaks with lemonade (the Brotherhood eschewed fermented liquors) and bought one raw for him; they distributed a few tracts, they let him chase thrown sticks around the field perimeter to his high delight, and Jenny danced a little when the teams joined in communal cavort. Would that all British youth spent its evenings so innocently.

They spoke not at all of the Reverend Mitten, his woman, and what to do about them. Not even when they were alone, throwing sticks for Herman. Deep beneath the conscious mind, thinking would have been going on; but to everything in life there is a season. A time to plan, a time to kill, a time to relax and let the hair down.

Mrs. Grebshaw was in no danger. The inspector, in common with all policemen nowadays, had come up against drugs before; he knew the difference between overdosed coma and the deep sleep of exhaustion that often follows a high. But that ambulance had to be sent for, there'd be trouble if it came out that he just let her lie there. She must be tagged by medics as drugged. So he covered her up, noting the flea-marks behind her knee, and had the little pastor come down with him to the telephone.

When the call was done he took the manikin back to the bedroom, where he said, because in the absence of support he could not deliver the official warning, "All right, little flower. Start talking."

"I don't know anything," said the Reverend Mitten. "I don't know anything." Panic in a deep voice sounds peculiar.

"You're a wicked little bastard," said Mr. Rosher. "That's what you are. Mind if I have a look round?"

In the short time before the ambulance arrived he found the syringe and the small package of drugs hardly hidden in the Reverend Mitten's bedside cabinet. Left there for a very short time only, the little man had

171

thought when he added to Mrs. Grebshaw's fleabites. Dead to rights, the little bastard. And more to come.

As soon as Mrs. Grebshaw had been carted away—she awoke when they lifted her onto the stretcher, but fell asleep again—he looked into Mrs. Filby-Stratton's room; and here he found the wires, almost invisible, stretched across from curtains to ceiling boss and back again, and the tape recorder that played him moans and cackles and evil whisperings; and in the wardrobe, plastic hands and a plastic skull, all tricked up with luminous paint.

It does not take long for a man steeped in experience of human depravity to work out two and two. "What I should do," said Inspector Rosher, "is put my foot straight through your bollix. I suppose you've got a will somewhere. Signed, is it, or were you still working on it?"

The little man was saying nothing now. This did not surprise the policeman. Here or at the station, he said to himself, I'll fillet the guts out of you, matie. Let's have a look at the rest of the house.

Nothing aboveground apparent to cursory inspection, but plenty could turn up when a squad dismantled that shrine and lifted all the floorboards and so on. And in the basement: delicate scales and a box of two thousand plastic envelopes. No drugs that he could see; but a quantity of French chalk. Dealers' equipment.

Proof positive! The grim corners of Mr. Rosher's leathery lips twitched momentarily upward at the sudden leap of his blood. Justification! He could string his story together now, he could point to spectacular result, nobody could jump on his back. Kudos! Kudos, and a bang in the snout for Grinly. A bloody drugs ring—you never know where it will lead. And the other business . . . Nothing about him, though, looked less than grim when he turned to the little man like a glaring gorilla and barked, "Where's your mate—the young feller from Chichester?"

"He's—not my—he's—out. They've gone—they've gone to the barbecue—"

Rosher knew of the barbecue. What he didn't know was—how many were involved? In drugs—in Harry's murder. Was their gathering a sort of dope-peddlers' convention, was the whole bloody dancing team bent? On the whole, he thought not—they had been performing expertly enough, so far as he could tell, when he saw them in the square. And the fat old trout with the begging bowl seemed clean, nattering away like women do about the lad who wasn't dancing because he didn't know the steps and the girl who was, because she did—learned since they joined the team, a matter of days ago. He glared upon the Reverend Mitten again and said, "How many of 'em are in this?"

"In what? In what?" said the little man.

"Don't fuck me about, Charlie," the gorilla barked. "You could sustain very nasty injuries, trying to escape. Now get up them stairs." And back they went to the upper regions, where the front door knocker sounded as they crossed the hall.

It was young Constable Dennison. He said, as soon as he was inside, "She died. The old lady. Died on the machine. At the hospital."

Festivities were still afoot when the Brotherhood team left the barbecue, early because they still had a service to attend back at the house. The young couple boarded with the rest and sat close together (it pleased them, sandwiched in this company, that he should have his hand down the back of her bright skirt, caressing her pretty

173

buttocks) on the coach-wide back seat with Herman at their feet, right above the case of heroin in the boot below; and they joined lustily in a mix of hymns and folk songs as the coach wended through darkening lanes to the main road, headed for home.

Some of the elation dimmed in Inspector Rosher. Could they—Grinly—anybody else—put in the boot over his not summoning an ambulance?

He said, "She was alive when you got her there?"

"Yes. They put her on oxygen but she died when they had her on the table." The young man was eyeing the Reverend Mitten with definite dislike, but it was Inspector Rosher who addressed the little man.

"Cockie, that's murder. That's a lifer, all on its own. I am arresting you for possession of drugs, and blah blah blah." Young Dennison knew the form. He was producing his notebook. "You do not have to say anything but I have to warn you that anything you do say will be taken down and may be used in evidence." One swift, unpunctuated sentence, slick with long use. He did not even wait for the man to speak. He turned his implacable eye to Constable Dennison and snapped, "Where's the car?"

"Out on the road."

"Get on the phone to the station. Tell 'em the situation—there's drugs here and evidence of extortion. Old lady full of drugs, Harry Grebshaw's wife gone to hospital, ditto. Old lady dead. Man calling himself Mutton arrested. When you've done that, whistle up the car. Tell 'em to get out of sight—into the field. Watch for the coach. Wait for further orders. I want you here with me."

Excitement was stirring in Constable Dennison. He actually felt the fighting man's pre-action kinship, directed to this tough, glowering gorilla. Say what you like about

174

the old bastard, he didn't specialize in dull moments. Something more was to come, and he was being bidden to participate. Wonder what it is? he thought as he crossed to the phone. Rosher spoke again.

"Tell 'em particularly to contact Mr. Grinly."

He was obeying a basic book-bending principle. Never phone in person. Use your underling to issue terse instructions, so that you do not find yourself voice-to-voice with the like of Grinly.

As a matter of fact, he did not have to worry at present about Mr. Grinly. Delivered home, that man stormed into the house in a foul temper. His wife, Mrs. Grinly, was in an equally volatile condition, she being a highly skilled cook and, like all artists, temperamental. Boiling already at having to ruin a good dinner by keeping it hot, she blew right back at him. In the enjoyment—it was mutual—of the subsequent row, she forgot to deliver Rosher's message.

18

They were still singing in the coach when it arrived at the gates of Pilbeam House. There was nothing to tell them the police were there, the place looked as usual; the squad car had withdrawn through a gate into the field and was hidden behind bushes. Apart from the young couple and the driver, none of them would have thought it significant had it been drawn up squarely in their path. They lifted up their innocent voices in a final burst of harmony as they were borne in through the gate and along the drive, while the Reverend Mitten sobbed like a baby inside the house, locked into a broom cupboard.

Mr. Rosher had put him there. It seemed the best thing. Nobody eyeing the inspector's implacable grimness would have suspected it—young Dennison certainly didn't—but the man was torn between normal enjoyment of adrenaline flow, addictive to a policeman as any drug, and unusual self-doubt.

Not that he feared anything that might come at him from the coach, when it arrived. He had in his time arrested mad men with choppers, naughty men with guns, Irish biddies liquored up and clawing outside pubs on St. Patrick's night—than which nothing is more terrible. Better a sawed-off shotgun.

No, no, no—nothing like that bothered him. On the contrary, this side of his work he always loved—the arrest, the handcuffing, the intoned warning; the sweep of that mighty hammer of fist with which God—who so far as he could see did not exist—had finished off his right arm, handy for when subject turned obstreperous.

What he doubted, now that it was too late, was whether he had done it right. He'd balanced himself on a very sharp razor's edge; and if anything went wrong, down he'd come, straddled. And there was a pretty prospect. It didn't bear thinking about.

But he did think about it. Hell—he was within touching distance of retirement; and in the short, tense time of waiting for the coach, he realized the full enormity to which simple murder had swollen.

A drugs distributor does not exist in isolation. Behind him is an international organization. And that means your actions come under the scrutiny of Scotland Yard— of Interpol—of the bloody Home Secretary, if it's big enough. And if you cock it up . . .

Oh, woe to the man who cocks it up, and bends the book to do it. "And why, Chief Constable, was a detective inspector operating alone in this matter, supported, it appears, only by a detective constable and one police car?"

Oo, bloody heck.

Almost, he had decided to ring the station himself—to call for full backing—because what if he was wrong, and everybody in that coach was bent? He actually began to twitch toward the phone.

Too late—too late. He heard the singing, he heard the

coach, and the self-doubt vanished in a new and mighty adrenaline-kick, as it vanishes in a boxer when the first bell sounds. That, or he gets clobbered. Rosher had never been clobbered.

He said to his detective constable, "Here it comes. We'll take 'em on the coach."

There would be a crush of bodies, stepping down and jostling about, once they began to alight. Better to board, calling upon them to keep their seats. If they did—they were clean. If not—easier to jump out, slam the door. Shut 'em in. Have the lot driven to the station under escort.

"Right," said Detective Constable Dennison. "Er—who are we after?" Because he still did not know.

"Young couple, specifically. Male and—" Now the penny dropped. The face—the girl—the pub. The night Harry was murdered. Only she'd been dressed unisex— jeans, jacket, kiss-me-sailor hat. But she wasn't a boy. "Male and female."

"Ah," said Constable Dennison, thinking: That's all right, so long as they're the only young couple. I suppose you know what you're doing. You'll be grabbing them, anyway.

Mr. Rosher was speaking again. "Right, then. I want us out and in that coach as soon as it stops."

This was happening in the hall, where he had elected to wait. He'd popped the Reverend Mitten into that lockable cupboard under the stairs just a minute or two ago, turning the key on him for safekeeping. He was out of the way in there, he couldn't scarper or get under the feet. He'd entered reluctantly, sobbing by now; not knowing, then or ever after—as neither did the police, for that matter—that this was, in fact, his lucky day. But for the intervention of events currently taking place, the lad

Tony would have had him for sure. As it was, he was safe for something like twenty years.

The events currently taking place proceeded as follows: Inspector Rosher and his peon crept into the porch from the hall with heads well down, through the door already opened and left like that to minimize visible movement. They were in position by the outer door when the coach drew up and stopped, whereupon the black hat came up suddenly, slightly preceding a fine head of hair, and the front door opened, and two large bodies moved rapidly toward the vehicle, one young and springy, the other with long arms swinging and posterior stuck out, bandying along at a fair old clip like a great ape fleeing a forest fire; and this one was barking loudly, "Keep your seats, please—stay where you are—"

He was a trifle late. Some people were up already, and issuing forth. There are always a few who crowd forward, ready to step down as soon as the doors open. Others, still rising, did not hear the cry at all because the singing was still going on. Not everybody saw the advancing bodies, and those who did had no reason to recognize them for what they were.

But Tony did. He knew the black hat. In no hurry to alight, he was still on the back seat between his Jenny and that fat lady who had rattled a collecting tin at Rosher; and he sat up with a jerk, saying, "Pigs! Pigs!"

"I beg your pardon?" said the fat lady, startled.

He made no answer. His eyes were turned to the window, watching the onward lope of the durable blue serge suit. The girl, whose head had dropped during the ride to his shoulder, sat up quickly beside him. At their feet the black dog tensed, feeling their sudden tensing.

It would, perhaps, have made no difference to the outcome had the policemen been able to step up into the coach unimpeded. Not when it is taken into account that the driver was an organization man, and he knew Rosher, having had him identified by the Reverend Mitten first time the inspector called; whereas Rosher did not know him. Take into consideration, too, that the driver knew what was in the boot—whereas Rosher knew nothing beyond the fact that he *might* be venturing among more bent than just the young couple.

Speculation. What boots it? The policemen could not board unimpeded. They ran into bodies, earthly wrappings of the radiant souls first out of the coach. Inspector Rosher plowed straight on, bruising toes, ribs, and two bosoms, separately owned; but Constable Dennison, bearing a handicap of manners inculcated by a loving mother, was inclined to say "excuse me" and to step around the impeding bulk, which once or twice stepped the same way, to execute with him the opening step of a good old-fashioned waltz.

Consequently, only Inspector Rosher was on board when the driver let his clutch in, to a motor still running because, as always, when the mugs were off he would take the coach on to park it beyond the house.

Now when the clutch is unexpectedly let in to a stationary coach, those standing inside tend to lurch about and stagger, falling into seated laps, clutching at each other, luggage racks, and the like, while those on the exit steps fall off, also clutching. The phenomenon may be viewed any day, at any rush-hour bus stop. So a lady already shouldered roughly by Inspector Rosher as he came aboard fell off the step with a shriek, clutched at Constable Dennison, who had just arrived there, and fell with him onto the gravel with a boggling display of Directoire knickers and another shriek. Before the constable had properly grasped what was happening, the coach was already half through the turn that would take it back to the gates, a wide arc over lawns and flower beds.

In it, the people staggered about, making no outcry because they were too surprised, but unable to steady themselves against the lurching turn. Among them Inspector Rosher staggered and shoved and tried to home in on his quarry, as surprised as anybody; while they, having only half risen, simply fell back on the seat. It upset the dog, though, having suddenly to scrabble for footing.

Out on the gravel, Constable Dennison's rising was hampered by the prostrate lady's clutching at his legs. He kicked clear, attained upright, and looked around for Inspector Rosher. No black hat among the ribboned headgear, no durable blue serge suit. Christ, he thought—he must be on it; and he fumbled for his personal radio. Before he established contact with the squad car lurking in a field, the coach was through the gate and on the road.

Madness, mayhap, to try to scarper in a coach; but panic often leads to the commission of crazy acts, and panic in the driver is what sent this one on its way. A useful man, but he lived on his nerves.

Maybe it was not entirely crazy, at that. He knew what was in the boot. He knew what was in the basement. He knew Rosher, he heard the shout, saw him and his policemanly consort hurrying. He knew why London had sent the young couple sitting on his back seat. He knew what they had done.

No—not altogether crazy. He was unaware of that squad car. If he could get to a distance—the city, where public transport is, and the railway station—the coach could be dumped in a quiet place of which he knew, with the dancers locked in; and they would give no trouble, he had a gun under the dashboard. Grab the suitcase, and the three of them could be off on their toes. Vanished.

181

Whether he thought all this out logically is very moot; but one thing every criminal mind knows instinctively, in this sort of situation: Staying, you are certainly lumbered. Going, you stand a chance. What he did not know, when he jabbed down on the accelerator, was that Rosher had scrambled aboard. Once the inspector barged into the press of bodies already alighted he was gone from sight. Precisely to prevent his and/or his acolyte's boarding, the driver pressed the button that hissed the doors to before he was properly into his turn. He did not realize the man was inside even when he staggered past. A dozen people were staggering, and he was busy steering between trees while fumbling under the dashboard for his gun.

It takes far longer to tell some things than it does for them to happen. The lurching, bumping turn back onto the drive from the flower-bed area sent everybody reeling sideways, some of them crying out by now. No sooner were they somewhat stabilized than braking at the gate had them tottering toward the driver's end. The turn onto the road restaggered them, and subsequent rapid acceleration set them going the other way, toward the back of the coach, with Rosher, in the lead, only just finding time to wonder about the driver.

This is when he came up against the dog.

In the field, the squad-car driver said to his oppo, "It's coming out again."

"What are we supposed to do?" his oppo said. "Follow it?"

"Didn't say so, did he? Get out of sight, he said. Stay here."

"Better stay, then," said the oppo, settling back in his seat. The coach was gone from sight again, their view through the bushes covering only the gate itself. At the inquiry later it was suggested that they should have been out among those bushes, keeping the whole road under obbo; but that was said with hindsight. Their instructions, as they pointed out very strongly, were merely to lie low and await further orders. Certainly, if they had got out, they'd have seen the coil of barbed wire. It blacked their career records badly, that they didn't.

No sooner was the oppo settled comfortably than the left-open radio spoke. Constable Dennison, crying, "Charlie Two—Charlie Two—"

The oppo clicked his microphone switch. "Charlie Two receiving," he said.

"The coach—gone off—Old Blubbergut's on it—"

"On it?"

"In it. It shot off—"

"Want it brought back?"

Constable Dennison, in truth, did not know what he did want, apart from somebody senior to tell him what to do, to shoulder the grimacing can. He was as astonished as anybody when the coach suddenly went. His brain, of course, was leaping all over the place. The young couple—killers? The old lady—drugs . . . Were they all bent, on that coach? The driver must be. Dangerous? Old Blubbergut on his tod—hostage? Guns? You never know, these days. "No—don't take it—follow it—buzz the station—Superintendent Grinly—they may be dangerous—"

"Right," said the oppo, as his driver switched on his engine. They knew what to do—raise the station, tell them the situation, keep them informed as to location of coach so that other cars could be diverted to converge. "Over?"

"Over," said Constable Dennison. He added, "—and out." He turned to the still shocked dancers, knowing by their very puzzlement that they were not bent, and so, presumably, nor were the others still on the coach—most of them—so were those who *were* bent rattling along with many more ready-made hostages than just Rosher? Oh, Jesus! He shouted above the excited babble. "Police. Quiet, please—QUIET! Everybody into the house—into the house—" Where the telephone is. This is too big for me—I want somebody out here.

The squad-car driver, pleased with promise of action to while away this late shift, swung the car backward exuberantly, twisting the wheel in his canny hands to full lock for the turn that would bring it facing the gate they'd come in by. Choose whether or not he was to blame.

The barbed-wire coil had been dumped among nettles, long-enough ago for them to have grown up around it. The first he knew of it was when they hit tarmac beyond the gate. A strange grating came from under the back. "What's that?" he wondered, and the car went bumpety-bump as a back tire flattened. They jumped out, he and his oppo.

What a calamity! Rusty barbed wire, caught in a great coil under the petrol tank, wrapped a-tangle round the near-side flat back tire. Well might he snatch off his cap and cast it from him, roaring, "Fuck it! Fuck it! Fuck it!"

"Where'd that come from?" his oppo wondered.

The rapid acceleration brought Mr. Rosher along the coach at a brisk totter. Behind him people clutched at luggage racks, seat backs, each other; but he was on his way to where he had spotted the young couple, sitting again on the back seat because they were still being collapsed back whenever they tried to rise. Also seated, and for the same reason, was the fat lady. And the dog, disturbed and having difficulty in holding position because a dog's pads were never designed to grip compo floors that sway and swing, was gamely obeying his master's last order.

In the back trouser pocket of the durable blue serge suit—ah, they don't make them like that anymore—were Mr. Rosher's handcuffs. He always carried them there. But no chance of his reaching for them as he tottered on toward the young man, who rose now, and grabbed the fat lady, and shouted, "Stay back! Stay back or I stick her!"

"No, Tony—no," the girl cried. He took no notice.

Rosher checked. Grabbed at a seat back and checked, two yards from the fat lady, whose eyes and mouth had popped wide open. The lad had tugged her to cover him. The dog was up, and growling. The young man shouted again.

"Sit down! Everybody sit down!" The dog, in a state of utter confusion by now, clutched at the familiar word and sat; but the lad flashed that thin, efficient knife briefly at Rosher and cried, "Get him, Herman!"

Difficult, to follow his reasoning. Presumably, he intended that he and the girl, and the driver, should leap out and scarper. A ravening Doberman at the throat of a black-hatted gorilla in a confined space must capture the attention of those confined with them, particularly when the communal mind does not know what's happening.

If that was his idea, it was poor thinking. The coach was still in the country, less than half a mile from where it had started. He should have made better use of his hostages, he had plenty of them. He should have consulted the driver, whose drive-into-the-city tactic was very much sounder so long as everybody kept their heads. Even if the police were homed on them, they could hardly attack a coach filled with holy innocents. Swap the fat lady for one or two bodies more maneuverable—demand a car— many a terrorist has done much more with much less.

But then, you see, it all happened so fast, with him and

the girl at one end of the coach, the driver at the other; and he never had been a really deep thinker. Active mind, yes. But never deep. Facile, and always running to violence, with a particular partiality for the knife. The girl might have done better, but she had no say in the matter.

So the dog Herman came at Rosher, happy to have a definite end to all this confusion. His doggy mind clicked down with relief to what he understood: order, and its execution. He leapt from sitting, going for the throat. Rosher staggered back along the coach, barking, "Gerroff, you bastard," one arm raised to defend the vulnerable windpipe.

Truly, they were marvelous value, those elephant-legged suits. What modern man-made fiber would stand between bone and the teeth of a Doberman pinscher? Blue serge will, if of mature-enough vintage. Rosher's did, all the way along the coach, with people not already seated plopping down and cringing to be out of the way. It never even tore. Closely examined later, it proved to be utterly unmarked.

The dog, be it admitted, did not actively savage it. He confined his snarling grip to one place—the left forearm, raised across the throat. This, no doubt, was because the target was unstable, staggering backward. Once it hit the front glass window with its backbone, a way would be found to richer meat. And down the aisle behind the dog came the young man propelling the fat lady, the pretty girl behind.

So, obviously, Tony's plan was to disembark and scarper. But the driver, having only his interior rearview mirror to aid observation, was not fully up with what was going on. There was a certain amount of screaming now, and the snarling of the dog. The driver kept his foot hard down, lickety-split for the big city; until the big blue body thudded against the glass observation-window-cum-wind-screen beside him, snarling back at the snarling dog attached by the teeth to its forearm.

Only now did that driver realize he had the copper on board. And he didn't have much time to ponder it. He had plenty to think about, like trying to get both hands to the wheel, one of them gripping a gun.

Now Mr. Rosher, too, had instruments that were unswerving to the very death, once orders arrived from that part of his brain more sure, more lightning-fast than thought; and chief among these was the Mighty Hammer, that awesome bunch of hairy right-hand knuckle, which swung now, a belt to the side of the head. Not altogether on target. The dog clung, slavering. And the coach raced on.

Not often that the Hammer missed its mark. Blame the donor's being off balance. Back to the wall, braced thereby, Rosher fired again, a fine, shortened hook that brought to the eyes of the dog an immediate squint; and another, even finer, which dislodged it completely, sending the black body flying straight onto the driver, into whom, doubtless too dazed to realize the target had changed, it sank its teeth and reclung.

The driver shot it. Perhaps inadvertently, but most effectively. It only needs shock to twitch the trigger finger.

He might have shot Rosher, too, all in a fresh panic, but he was pretty busy; because what with shock, dog bite, and the heavy black body slumping down around his gear levers, pedals, feet, bumping his arm on the way down, he dropped the gun to grapple the wheel; but the coach had lurched out of control.

Mayhem, now. Seconds only, but in terms of experience, packed to the very brim.

The coach lurched with a screaming of tires. It must have been doing seventy. Miles per hour, not Common Market kilometers. It rocked, on one side the wheels lifted. People screamed, grabbed, clutched, none palpably resting in God. The fat lady—oh, and she was lucky—plunged sideways and head-first into a seat, shrieking like a marmoset as her collarbone snapped, Tony too occupied himself to slip in the knife or to do anything about it. The girl behind him clutched at a luggage rack, Rosher grabbed the rail beside the sobbing driver's seat, the floppy dog against his lower legs; and the coach shot with inches to spare between trees, straight through the roadside fence.

Now on the far side of that fence, rimmed only with a stand-off of barbed wire, is an old worked-out quarry. Not immediately adjacent, you cover twenty flat yards before you reach it. Twenty yards is not a lot, and barbed wire may stop a police car, but it does nothing for a runaway coach.

Rosher, through the big window, grasped the essentials at once. If it was a prayer, his was the only one that went up as the coach plowed on. "Oo Christ," he said, and clutched again as the driver, ash-faced and bolt-eyed, managed to kick a foot clear and jam it on the brake pedal, fighting the wheel to slew the coach round.

He succeeded. Just and only just. Sideways onto the very rim of a fifty-foot drop the vehicle halted; but the confusion went on. People screaming, the fat lady in hysterics, the pretty girl bleeding at the nose, swinging from the luggage rack behind the young man, who was reeling with his hands clasped to his skull, having cannoned head-first into a window and back again at the final slewing. He still held the knife.

Policemen, though they wear an exterior dead ringer for a gorilla, have within them something of the spirit of the British bulldog, or the Doberman pinscher. Given an objective, they cleave unto death. And Rosher undoubtedly did the right thing. You cannot leave a wounded killer standing among a batch of screaming innocents, armed with a sharp knife.

He let go his grip and lurched forward. The Mighty Hammer swept again. Almost before the knife went clatter-clatter harmlessly among the rear seats he was dropping the sagged body of the lad and looking for trouble from the pretty girl, glaring out of little red eyes.

She was giving no trouble. When she relinquished grip on the luggage rack she fell to the ground and crouched there, hands over her broken nose and sobbing.

It was the driver who opted for out. Bruised, battered, and bitten, he'd had no time to refasten his seat belt, so he'd bounced with the rest—and with judgment seriously impaired, he hissed the doors open while groping the floor for the gun. He never found it, because of the dog.

That dog was not dead. Stunned by Rosher's heavy fist, slammed vitally by a bullet; but not yet dead. It opened those squinty eyes and there was a hand, groping. Poor, bemused beast, it sank the fangs in.

The driver came out of his seat with a screech and threw himself toward the door; but he had to get over Herman, who—surely there is a place for dogs in heaven?—faithful in love to the last, even as his eyes glazed over, clamped on at the ankle. Convinced, of course, that this confused eruption threatened his two beloved.

"Gerroff—gerroff!" yelled the driver, kicking clear and half falling through the exit door.

There was no footing at all on that side of the coach, it virtually overhung the quarry. A fifty-foot fall head-first onto slate slab does the skull no good at all. Such a spectacular end deserves better than that those left behind do not even hear the short scream and the bonk.

They were screaming themselves, and several—all of them, perhaps, like terrified lemmings—might well have followed him over, because they were beginning in stark panic to struggle from their seats, and people in panic, they want out from where the problem is. And here let us pay tribute, not specifically to Inspector Rosher, but to that fine, disciplined body of men, the British police.

This one, battered and shaken himself, realized again the potential of the situation. The barrel chest expanded, the hairy-male voice rang out. Any policeman would have done it, tenor, baritone, or basso profundo. There are few countertenors in the Force.

"Stay where you are! Keep your seats! Keep your seats!"

And do you know, so great is the authority behind the police voice, so ingrained the British habit of obedience to it, even in this day of riot and brick-slinging, that they did as they were bloody well told.

19

The Chief Constable was still in his dinner jacket, having left his big-city glittering knees-up as soon as the station's call reached him. He drove straight to the quarry. Very distingué. It was a beautiful suit, although it would never wear like Mr. Rosher's. Nobody would have suspected the touch of dyspepsia under it, caused by a summons to mayhem involving Rosher immediately after the rather cheeky little wine that had accompanied the lobster thermidor. He braced his belly against it and said, "The media will be having a field day."

It would. A TV news crew had arrived already, and reporters were ringing the station. The buzz was out that something tasty was afoot with Rosher mixed into it; and Rosher always gave value.

The Chief was addressing Superintendent Grinly, without looking at him. Mr. Grinly's normal lugubriosity had turned evil, the nostrils tending to flare and twitch. When he answered, it grated between snarl and snap.

"No doubt, sir. No doubt."

Good reason for this new savagery. Consider his position. Nobody had yet asked him in so many words how come Inspector Rosher was involved alone, how come by the time he arrived himself, speeding to the site after the station telephoned—he still did not know of Rosher's earlier message, his wife disdained now to tell him—everything was over except for the last of the ambulances bumping out to the road and a party of policemen fetching up from the quarry the driver's body.

Nobody asked in words; but it was in the eyes, and it would be in all the reports. His own included. Even Rosher had departed, riding herd on his prisoners, to the hospital, where, by the book, he must himself be checked for injury and such injury noted or not, according to whether he had any. Mr. Grinly had been forced to stay, station radio having reported that the Chief was on his way.

The Chief spoke again. "There were no serious injuries, you say?"

"Broken collarbone, broken nose," snapped Mr. Grinly. "Cuts and abrasions. Shock. That's all, according to the doctor's preliminary report. Apart from the driver. He's dead." And still lying about, covered with a plastic sheet. A police pathologist was bending over him even now.

"Fortunate," the Chief said, obviously not referring to the driver. He looked at the coach. "Miracle it didn't go over." That would really have set a covy of cats slavering among the pigeons. Think of the TV pictures. A smashed coach and bodies, akimbo for preference. Or trapped inside, and burning. Such stuff as media dreams are made on.

Fortunate indeed the people in that coach had been. Had there not been an emergency exit on the fieldward

192

side, Rosher could never have bullied them out; and the movement of hysterical bodies within might well have tumbled it. The Chief's eyes were on it. He said, "It could still go. Can we brace it? Tow it back a little?"

"Might be able to drive it."

"I wouldn't want to put a man in. Do we have tow ropes?"

Squad cars were here now, on the road and one in the field, set there for instant relaying of radio messages. They'd all have tow ropes, but not designed for coach hauling. Neither are police cars. If the thing slipped, they could easily be hauled over with it. A tug-of-war setup was in the Chief's mind, strong men ready and willing to jump clear in a hurry. Mr. Grinly said, "I doubt if they'd cope with that. I've got a heavy recovery vehicle on its way."

Heavy recovery vehicles bumble along, you cannot rush them. And the coach was in imminent danger. "What about the thing itself?" said the Chief. "Surely they carry something suitable?"

Mr. Grinly shouted a brief order. One of the hovering policemen went toward the boot.

In the cottage hospital, uniform men stood guard over the two prisoners, both of whom were in bed; the lad concussed, the girl in shock with her pretty nose swollen blue and broken, blackened eyes desperately weeping for her dog. In a general ward, less blatant watch was kept over the more dramatically hysterical of the Christians, who had been stuck with a quick needle and popped into bed. The less affected were having names and addresses noted while they sipped at warm, well-sweetened tea. They must all be interrogated before they left.

193

Mr. Rosher had been examined, and bruising found upon the cranium. He must have clouted it on something. They passed him as not likely to succumb, and rightly. That skull was as durable as the suit, and well protected by the black hat. A dab of some unction, and they said he could go home. The dog had left no mark.

But go home he could not. He must wait there until Grinly—the Chief—somebody—arrived. He must wait there and worry. It never occurred to him to give thanks that he was not lying mangled among the mangled at the bottom of a disused quarry.

As that uniform man approached the boot and opened it, the Chief said, "It means a full inquiry, of course."

"Of course, sir," Mr. Grinly snapped. He knew bloody well it did. He knew what it meant. Blots all round. And he still was not sure how it all had happened. Wasn't even sure what was happening.

Everything was garbled: the little parson arriving there handcuffed, in care of young Dennison, driving Rosher's car, who also seemed to know nothing except that the old lady was dead and Grebshaw's wife in hospital, doped to the eyeballs; that Rosher—sod Rosher! sod him! sod him! sod him!—had arrested this little man and locked him in a cupboard before boarding the coach, which had shot off, leaving the young twat standing. And a squad car stood outside Pilbeam House, twisted about with barbed wire, of all things. Mr. Grinly sent the constable off to the station, to book the little man in. Nobody even knew exactly for what, until Rosher was available to clarify.

Small wonder that these two responsible policemen stood chewing their (metaphorical) mustaches in silence now, as the boot was raised, the floor section concealing

194

the spares-and-tools well lifted; and a general shout went up. "Look out! Look out!"

The man at the boot jumped back. Bully for him that he did, because the earth had crumbled at last. Given way, and the coach was on the move. The TV crew wept with joy, getting lovely pictures.

And that is how they discovered the suitcase. Burst open in the burst boot, packets all around among the wreckage. And that is when the worries besetting the Chief and his superintendent deepened, as into their minds loomed Scotland Yard, Interpol, the Home Office, because this was not a few grams of cannabis. Somewhere back of this were very big boys.

Mr. Rosher, when he finally left the hospital, did so in obedience to direct summons. He was to return to the station. Report to the Chief Constable in his office. Pausing only for a quick flip to the toilet, and to adjust his dress before leaving, he had himself driven through town in one of the two cars waiting in the hospital driveway.

When he arrived, he found his beat-oppo from happy days long ago on duty at the reception desk. His name was Barney Dancey. Sergeant Barney Dancey. Blessed are the pure in heart, and he was one. All his working life in a police force and still the bonny blue eye beamed with childlike faith. Amazing. Grew chrysanthemums. To him, Rosher said, "What goes on, Barney?"

"Buggered if I know, Alf." Only man in all the world who addressed Mr. Rosher by his forename. Only man in the world to whom Mr. Rosher attached a forename.

If Barney didn't know, nobody did. "The Old Man back?"

"On his way. Your lady's in with the drugs lads. Number four." The interview-room number.

"What lady?"

"A Mrs. Blenkiron."

"Ah." He'd forgotten all about her.

"And young Dennison brought your little feller in. He's down in the cells. Singing, they reckon. Bertie Harris is in with him. And the Dennison lad."

Something of magic in the way Barney got to know these things. Nobody had come up from the cells to tell him, but he knew the Reverend Mitten was singing. Already Detective Superintendent Harris, called hastily in the absence of Mr. Grinly to conduct the flow of melody, knew the facts behind the murder of Harry Grebshaw, the truth about the old lady. He knew about a suitcase in the coach boot—didn't know it was lying with contents scattered amid the wreckage in the quarry—and was working to obtain addresses in London and the States. He didn't get any, because the little man had none; but a phone number proved very useful to Scotland Yard later.

"Uh-huh," said Rosher, wondering if he dare go down to sit in on the interrogation. But better not. Better wait for the Old Man, as ordered.

"Blew wide open, this one," Barney said, "didn't it?"

"Herrumph," said Rosher. He produced a slate-gray handkerchief that would have been snow-white in the days when the fat wife presided over the washing machine. The sergeant braced himself.

As the echoes died away, a uniform squad driver came with his oppo from the corridor along which are the four interview rooms, side by side. Walking plump between them was Mrs. Blenkiron. When she saw the inspector, she said, "Ah—Mr. Rosher—am I arrested? I've been asking all the time to see you but they said you were out."

"Rmph," he said. "Mrs.—er—" He tucked the gray sheet away. Even now, a tiny piece of her feminine eye noted the color, her needful mind whispered, he needs looking after, really.

"Blenkiron," she said. "Molly Blenkiron. Only nobody seems to know what I am supposed to have done. I mean—I told you about my sister, and—you sent your policemen in front of all the neighbors, and—I've been sitting in that room—and now they've come and they're taking me to the hospital. It's my sister—she's in hospital—"

"I know, madam," said Rosher.

"They asked me about—I've told them all I know—" But not quite all. She'd had sense enough to hold back the fact that she flushed her sister's happy gear down the loo. She did it for her sister's sake rather than her own; but she did herself a favor. So long as she kept her mouth shut—what had they to charge her with? If anybody wanted to charge her. "Did they try to murder her?"

"Who?"

"Well—I was watching the telly, and this man said they stop at nothing—"

She spoke on, but the inspector was not listening. The door in from the street opened with a bang and the Chief Constable had arrived, together with Superintendent Grinly, who wore the face of a pantomime demon. It was unlike the Chief Constable to offer discourtesy to a member of the female public, at any time or anywhere; but he ignored Mrs. Blenkiron completely, speaking right through her. And very curtly. "My office, Mr. Rosher, if you please."

Without breaking stride, the two seniors were away, up the stairs. Mrs. Blenkiron's speech flow had checked, she looked round to see who had spoken. Mr. Rosher said,

"These officers will take care of you, madam," and he bandied across the reception hall to mount in their wake, head well down between the formidable shoulders.

In the wide blue eyes of Mrs. Blenkiron, wistfulness lingered as she watched him go. She didn't know what was happening, and of course you couldn't call him handsome. But she did like a man who was a man.